CW00722279

Secrets and Lies

The Plymouth Writers Group

Published in 2017 by FeedARead.com Publishing

Copyright © The authors as named: Sarah Adams, Charles Becker, Julie Birkett, Mary Curd, John Curry, Elaine Dorr, Louis Fletcher, Alan Grant, John L. Horsham, Moyra MacKyan, Mary McClarey, David Shannon, Mary Thomas, Douglas Bruton, Sheila Blackburn, Grant Price, Erik Lofroth, Richard Hooton

First Edition

The authors have asserted their moral right under the Copyright, Designs and Patents Act, 1988, to be identified as the author of this work.

All Rights reserved. No part of this publication may be reproduced, copied, stored in a retrieval system, or transmitted, in any form or by any means, without the prior written consent of the copyright holder, nor be otherwise circulated in any form of binding or cover other than that in which it is published and without a similar condition being imposed on the subsequent purchaser.

Sebastian Kennell, who excelled as a student of Trudi Port at St Austell College, designed the cover for this Anthology as the winner of a small competition. His artistry, understanding of design principles and expertise in Photoshop resulted in an `aesthetic intrigue`, drawing the reader into the essence of the written word in this latest edition of the Plymouth Writers Group's collection of creative writing.

Contents

Competition Winners

Highly Commended

The Chairman's Foreword.

This is the fourth annual anthology of the work of members of the Plymouth Writers' Group, and the theme 'Secrets and Lies' has created a huge range of responses.

In a departure from our other productions, each writer was given a limit of 4,500 words to be used in whatever way they wished, along with the total responsibility for editing their own work. So you know who to blame for any mistakes!

PWG is now in its eleventh year and we hope you'll not only enjoy looking for familiar names, but also the work of exciting new writers appearing for the first time.

In keeping with previous years we are also delighted to include the first five winners of our annual international writing competition.

On a sad note: we were sorry to learn that one of our absent friends, Mike Green, has been placed on a seriously ill list. Mike is well known in the Plymouth area for his input to poetry and prose, and has performed at many 'open mic' and 'stand-up events.' I have been in touch with Mike and spent time with him. It is my pleasure to announce that Mike was offered an Associate Membership to our group - in recognition of his services to writing - and has happily accepted.

The group is in good shape and, because of time constraints at our monthly meetings, it sadly has had to turn away prospective members.

Finally, The Plymouth Writers' Group is proud of its continuing association with the University of Plymouth's English and Creative Writing Department.

Happy Reading,

Lou Fletcher
Chairman.

LIES AND SECRETS

By Sarah Adams

Our span of days has come and gone, good and bad in their allotted measure, as everyone's days fall. No more berries would ripen; our stories would spin away from us, mostly lost on dusty shelves, a few claiming a future to be told and re-told.

The time you ate pot-pourri at a 1970's family "do", mistaking it for some new-fangled nibbles. When we swam near naked, drunk, who knows whose party or pool it was, and somehow didn't drown. When the kids roamed the end of the festival throwing aerosols onto lingering fires, and not a singed eyebrow between them. (We would have hurled the Health and Safety book at them, had we known).

But when you stroked my palm to soothe my nighttime terrors; and learned to love, even encourage, my guinea-pig obsession; the hours I spent entranced by the elusive gold in your hazel eyes or caught you crying at your first ballet, those stories are gossamer. Time's breath has dandelioned them to the edge of nowhere. As with the sunken iceberg of stories, of the sunken iceberg of the mass of us, barely a tip impacts on anything at all. It seems that our goals and lists and inconsistencies turn to ashes , as those two great thieves Time and Age creep unnoticed into us and inevitably win the day.

And the stories we told each other – well, some came true. That we would one day watch whales under the frozen, fairy skies of the furthest North; that was a happy ever after. That we would make a decent loaf of bread (a year-long saga, but eventually we triumphed). That Facebook wouldn't taint us – well, that was a story with alternating endings.......

Our recurring theme was the story of that future golden day, to be celebrated with the most cherished friends we had gathered up through the years. We would board a grand steam train and ride in great style with sumptuous food through our glorious, beloved English countryside. But that story, in the end, was a lie. Two months, one week, and three days short of the truth. That our born-to-soon baby son would live and grow and flourish and see many sights: that was a lie too. He was four days old; he only knew the incubator.

Venice and Rome: truths. Hawaii and Route 66: lies. Surviving three heart attacks: a miraculous truth. Next year, eat less cake: hmm....... all lies! We hadn't really meant to lie, our dreams just ran away with us sometimes. And now, you had run away from me. You didn't want to, but the full-stop at the end of your story was solid and dry on the page. So almost all our stories, the fake and the factual, fade. Three children are not enough shelf space, nor eight grandchildren, nor all those cousins, nieces, nephews, spouses. (I will never again know their many names).

Farewell my love. The story was still worth the telling. The world is better for it, though it will soon be the faintest echo. Lies are sometimes just dreams that lost their strength or got forgotten when we woke. Fight for some of your truths to the bittersweet end, that's all.

BUTTERFLY

by Sarah Adams

Fly soft away jewelled butterfly
Spread your wings and paint the sky
Let my spirit soar with you
Into endless smiling blue.
Up where rainbows promise gold
Up where children's dreams are told.
Down below spreads wide the world
With all its secrets to be learned.

How the hare knows when to box
Swift grey, moonlit shadow unlocked.
Where the owl on silent wing
A hooked and silent death may bring.
How an oval nail-sized seed
Ten centuries of bark and trunk can feed.
How a flower can tell the time
And why a flower is a lion.

How grass becomes both body and milk,
Why breezes sing upon the hill.
Why dear Humpty had his fall,
What lies beyond that mossy wall.
Why the lady's house burnt down,
Or why the blackbird's wife is brown.
Why no-one knows what path's ahead,
Or where my footsteps may be led.

How this fragile butterfly
Has strength to dare the farthest sky?
And when these secrets I've come to know,
A child no more, will I still grow?

DUCK, HERE COMES DONALD

by *Sarah Adams*

And so the world woke
Considerably wackier
With his hilarious haranguing
And nonsensical name
A terrifying transparency
That has, in the end,
Won him the day.

When a liberal, younger, coloured hope
Did not deliver;
When a rival reeks of deceit
And a slimy, surreptitious past;
When the global mind underestimates
(unbelievably, for it is an old, old device)
The power of polemic -

Well then, the way lies open
For such a man.
Forceful, fearsome, finance-driven
Now our leader - of the free(?) world
So, duck everyone,
You'd better duck!
For here comes:

Deceptively devious
Dangerously dark
Way-out......but now, oh Lordy,
Way way in.
Waddling
About turn, about turn, about turn,
No friend of Mickey
DONALD

10

Lonesome Larry

by *Charles Becker*

His mother had called him Lawrence till the end, even with her dying breath. "My beautiful Lawrence," she whispered and was gone. In 1939, she had fallen in love with Lawrence Olivier, as Heathcliff in the film of Wuthering Heights, with a longing that never faded. But, to the rest of his family and to all his friends, he had always been 'Larry'.

Even now in his early 70s, he still felt like a Larry, rather than a Lawrence. He thought he would have to dress in trousers with creases and wear a trilby to be a Lawrence. Just saying the word sounded stuffy and required a more formal shaping of the mouth; whereas, he could say Larry with a smile.

As he entered his local Co-op, glad to be out of the wind and the rain, he stepped to one side near the baskets, away from the flow of other shoppers. He pushed back the hood on his jacket and unzipped it, took off the curved sunglasses he wore to protect his weakening eyes and slid them into his inside pocket; then, he pulled off his gloves – strangler's gloves he called them, because they were tight, dark leather – and stuffed one in each side pocket.

He paused, thinking how free of all these encumbrances he had been in his youth and how long all this winter rigmarole took him now. He still felt young on the inside; it was just his body that seemed to disagree a lot of the time. He took off his denim cap, folding the peak in on itself, and angled it into the hip pocket of his jeans. Finally, he fumbled under his sweater for the bifocals in his shirt pocket and put them on.

Taking a basket from the stack, he hesitated before moving forward, trying to remember the list of things he needed. All he could think of was the bottle of sparkling wine he was going to buy. And the thought immediately lifted his mood. He had a date, a date

11

with Anna Alder. They had never met before, but they had spoken on the 'phone a few times and he was excited about meeting her. He made directly for the chiller unit near the tills and reached for a bottle of the orange-labelled Prosecco he'd tried before.

"Larry, you're 72 years old, you're half-deaf, half-blind and half-demented; or, at least, you forget what you're trying to remember most of the time." It was at that point he remembered the paper, lemons and toothpaste he wanted. He turned back into the aisles grinning, as the internal cataloguing of his defects continued. "You've got boozer's veins across your cheeks, a wonky knee, an inner tube round your belly and you're a slap head! Don't get your hopes up, sunshine!"

It was true; his hopes were up. He'd been on his own a long time. Almost twenty years now since Jacky had left. He tossed a lemon into the basket and skirted a couple of aisles looking for the pharmacy shelves. In one way, he didn't blame her. He knew he'd become depressed and withdrawn after his redundancy, while the bloke she'd met skiing was on the up. Something to do with computers. Or was it mobiles? It didn't matter. She wanted the good life more than she wanted him. He despised her for it, and his anger was full of hurt.

"All available hands to the checkout!" a harassed voice cried out over the speakers.

The toothpaste selection confused him: 'Pro Gum Health', 'Whitening', 'Daily Repair', he wanted all of those. In the end, he reached for 'Triple Action'. It promised 'fresh breath' and, in the circumstances, he decided that might be more important than anything-else.

As he queued to pay, the mocking voice started up again; "Shouldn't you be thinking of companionship rather than bonking at your age? Besides, you'd probably not rise to the occasion, anyway!"

"Next!"

He shuffled forward and plonked his basket on the counter. It was the friendly, weary woman he liked.

"Morning, love. Got a Co-op card?"

"Yes, but not with me."

It was another small defeat. He carried the few items to an empty service counter, slipped off his rucksack, loosened its neck and pushed them in. Then, while freeing his cap and flipping it on with one hand, he stuffed his spectacles back into his shirt pocket, with the other. Ready to leave, he zipped up his coat, but immediately had to unzip it again to get his sunglasses out. Finally, fishing for the trailing shoulder-strap of his rucksack, he headed for the exit, pausing when he got there to tug his hood up and pull on his gloves. That was when he realized he'd forgotten the paper.

*

Later on, towards half-past three, he set off for Anna's house, with the chilled bottle wrapped in newspaper heavy in his rucksack. It was a twenty minute walk, mainly up-hill, to Gladstone Terrace where she lived, and he hoped the wine would still be cold by the time he got there. The narrow road rose steeply and he paused at intervals, turning each time to find more and more of the harbour and bay below emerging from behind the screen of clustered buildings and rooftops. Feeling anxious about what she would make of him, he was reassured to some extent, as the rain petered out and the brightening sky over the horizon to the west slowly spread towards him.

Would they be compatible, he wondered. And what did that mean? He knew he was more tolerant these days of other people's views and foibles; so, why shouldn't she be? Trustworthiness and a sense of fun were what he valued most, and he had sensed both those qualities in her from the conversations they'd had

At the brow of the hill, he turned off up a gravel path running in front of a terrace of colourfully painted Edwardian houses, with bay windows facing out to sea and short front gardens. Wanting to compose himself, he stopped by the gate with a brass 9 on it and studied the house two doors further on. Number 11 was sage green, its faded slate roof daubed with brilliant splashes of mustard lichen, as the full blare of the sun chased the last of the shadows from it.

Even as he watched, the front door drew back and out of the shaded interior stepped a tall woman, who waved to him and stood waiting with her arms folded. Her gate was open; and, as he turned

13

in between the stone pillars and up the flagstone path towards her, she gave him a broad smile. "Hello, Larry. I saw you from the window and thought maybe you'd forgotten the number."

"I was just taking in the view," he said, stopping a couple of feet short of her. He felt unnerved. She was so different from how he had imagined her; not fine and dark and orderly, but relaxed and ramshackle and expansive, with a loose shirt over baggy trousers and strands of ginger-red hair streaked with silver escaping from whatever was gathering the rest of it behind her.

She stepped down and kissed his cheek, putting a strong arm around his shoulders. "Welcome," she said. "Come on in." And, turning to lead the way, she went back inside.

*

The house was lighter and more spacious than his own, with a broader hall and staircase. The ceilings were higher too, he realized, as he followed her into a large, airy room that had been knocked through and now ran from one end of the house to the other, with a bay window at the front and patio doors at the rear. It was a comfortable room, full of fabric and colour and mess, with a surprising baby grand piano against the far wall, half-way to the bay.

"I still give lessons," she said, following his eye.

He smiled and nodded and searched for something to say to her, then remembered the sparkling wine. "Oh, yes," he said, slipping off his rucksack and opening it; "I brought this for you." He gripped the neck of the bottle and pulled it free from the newspaper. "I hope it's still cold enough. I thought maybe we could... that is, that you might like..." He held it out to her.

"Did you?" she laughed, taking it. She looked at the label. "How lovely! Thank you. I'll put it in the fridge and we can have some later. But first we're going to have some tea and a good old chinwag. So, give me your jacket and make yourself at home, while I put the kettle on."

After she left him, he wandered over to the piano to look at the photographs arranged there. A crowd of faces looked back at him, all unfamiliar, except for one. Catching his breath, he reached out for the monochrome portrait in a silver frame of a young woman

14

with dark hair. As he gazed at the familiar face, a flood of affection surged through him. He carried her near the window and sat down. How could she be here! It made no sense.

When, eventually, Anna returned carrying a tray, he was aware of her; but he was unwilling to look up, until she spoke. "Come and help yourself," she said; "and there's carrot cake, if you'd like some."

She cleared a space for the tray by the sewing machine on the table, in the other half of the room. As he neared her, he held out the photograph. "Anna, who is this?" he said. "I mean I know who she is, but who is she to you?"

She snatched the frame from him, holding it close against her chest. "That's private!" she said.

He felt the chill of her rebuff, like a slap. His face was hot, but he couldn't let it go. "She's my aunt," he said. "Well, she was. She died while I was still at school." The words caught in his throat and he paused, swallowing hard. "She was my mum's younger sister...Aunty Grace."

Anna pulled out a chair and slumped into it. She held the photo away from her in her lap and looked down at it, then clasped it to her again with both hands.

"Please," she said, indicating the chair beside her; and her grey-blue eyes followed him, as he sat down; but their focus was far away and he waited.

"You've taken me by surprise," she said at last, placing the photo face-up between them on the table. She breathed in deeply and straightened her back. "This is in confidence; it's not something I talk about. But, if this really is your aunt, then you need to know."

The air was changed. This wasn't a date anymore. Something weightier than hopeful expectation was hanging between them, and he both did and didn't want her to go on.

"My parents presented me with this photograph on my twenty-first birthday." Her eyes were fully alive to him now. "Apparently, the orphanage gave it to them, when they adopted me. I was three months old." She took hold of the frame and tilted it. "Your Aunt Grace is my birth mother. I never knew her name before."

15

Larry sat, shaking his head from time to time, trying to remember something that would make sense of what she'd just told him; but he couldn't. "Nothing was ever said," he told her. "Nothing."

"Too much shame in those days, I suppose," Anna said. "Poor Grace!" She leant forward, placing her hand on his; and the warmth of her touch ignited the longing for contact in him. "It means you're family, Larry...real family!" She was smiling at him through her tears. "We're cousins!" she said, curling her fingers into his and gently squeezing them. "How extraordinary is that!"

"No bedroom boogie, then?" jeered his tormentor; but Larry didn't care.

"I'm so glad I came today," he said. "I nearly chickened out."

The Box File

by *Charles Becker*

"Well, I'm not keen on en suites," Laura said, smiling at us and then glaring at her husband, number three. "Patrick lets rip so loudly first thing every morning, the tooth mugs fall over. And the smell...!" She waved her hand in front of her face.

Patrick finished his mouthful and dabbed his lips with a napkin. "And, of course, no such pestilential airs ever pass between your cherubic cheeks, my sweet, do they?"

Laura raised her eyebrows at him and laughed. "Sounds like you've got a dictionary stuck between yours?"

"Now, children, no squabbling," said Natalie, Laura's oldest friend from school, reaching for the wine bottle and refilling our glasses.

"You could try *blu tack* on the tooth mugs," I offered, hoping to deflect their escalating swordplay.

Patrick, however, was not yet ready to yield. "You surprise me," he said, knitting his brows in apparent concern; "I thought those were normal, quotidian words. I didn't mean to confuse you."

I ought to explain that Laura's my cousin. I've known her all my life; and, generally, I try to avoid getting involved in her marital contests. But, I've always rather fancied Natalie, even when she was married and it was hopeless. There's a sassy kind of mischief about her that just does it for me. In fact, I'd only gone along to this Sunday lunch, because I knew she was going to be there. But I was already beginning to regret it.

"Bollocks!" Laura said, as she started to clear away our plates, scraping leftovers onto the top one, as she did so.

"Must you?" Patrick's irritation was clear. "Surely, the vulgar bangarang of stainless steel on china is better confined to the kitchen." He turned to me. "Don't you think so, Ben?"

Happily, before I could reply, Natalie winked at me and intervened: "Bangarang! What a wonderful word! Wherever does it come from?"

"The crossword in the Telegraph, of course." Laura said, rattling the cutlery against the plates as she passed him. "That's where all his big words come from." She paused, looking at us. "He left school at fifteen. The crossword's his self-education, isn't it, Patrick? Go on, tell them. There's nothing to be ashamed of."

And, satisfied with having had the last word, she disappeared.

*

The following evening, I was at home watching a world title fight I'd recorded, my mouth full of baked potato, when the 'phone rang. It was Natalie.

"Hi, Ben. Is this an okay time?"

"Yes, fine," I spluttered, pausing the boxing and carrying my plate through to the oven.

"Are you eating?"

Holding the receiver against my leg, I spat the remaining mush into the sink. "Just finished," I said.

"Thing is, Ben, I don't know how you feel; but, ever since lunch yesterday, I've been wondering what to do about Laura and Patrick."

I wasn't sure if her pause was an invitation for me to respond or whether she'd stopped for a puff on her cigarette.

Playing safe, I said: "It'd be good if we could help." The naturalness of the 'we' excited me. "But do you think Patrick's right for her? I mean he seems...I don't know...so pompous."

"It's a defence," she said, as I wandered back into the other room and switched off the table lamp. I like talking in the dark; it brings the other person closer. And I wanted Natalie closer.

"A defence?"

"Yes. And Laura's the same. She always ridicules the man she's with...you know that."

"I certainly do!" I said,

Natalie laughed...well, it was more of a conspiratorial giggle really, warm and breathy. "Ah, so you've been on the receiving end, as well! And that's the point, isn't it?"

There was another pause; and this time I waited.

"It's a defence, just like Patrick's windbagging. That's my theory, anyhow. They both love each other, but neither of them can risk

18

showing it. Make them too vulnerable. So, they fight instead. You know, like a boy in the playground pulling the plaits of a girl that's caught his eye."

"I wish I'd pulled *your* plaits." In the safety of the dark, I'd spoken my thought aloud without intending to.

There was an ominous silence. I stopped breathing and my throat turned to sand.

"Maybe, we should meet," she said eventually, "and talk this over."

Bluebells sprang where there were none. "That would be great," I said, breathing out again.

*

After the call, I was on a high; and I'd only just put the receiver down, when it cried out again. It was Laura and she was using that *I'm-older-and-more-experienced-than-you* tone she often adopts with me.

"I'm just ringing about yesterday. I'm sorry Patrick was so awful. I don't know what's the matter with that man. He's not like that, when we're on our own. Anyway I've told him, if it happens again, he'll have to go. I don't know what you and Nat must have thought. I tried her just now, but the line's engaged."

Putting Natalie's theory to the test, I said: "Do you think he does it, because he's afraid of showing how much he...you know...cares about you?" Put this way, I wondered if the penny might drop for her, too; but it didn't sound like it had.

"Probably. He's no good at showing his feelings. I don't know if I've told you before, but he had a tough childhood; no father, and a mother who never showed him any affection. Everything he's achieved, he's done entirely by himself."

Her growing tone of approval began to give me some understanding of what had drawn her to him. Treated by my uncle, her father, as a pretty blonde in need of a good husband rather than a good education, she, too, had had to make her own way in the world.

I told her there was no need to apologise, thanked her for the lunch and said I hoped they could sort things out.

19

"Don't worry; I'll sort him out, all right!" She gave her combative laugh and rang off.

The two calls left me elated on one count and hopeful on the other; and I certainly had no inkling of the tragedy that was about to follow, or of the tenderness.

*

Easter came and went, and Natalie and I met quite a few times *to talk about Laura and Patrick*, which became our code for getting together. We never quite cracked their problem, but we had a lot of fun demonstrating the virtues of being naked and vulnerable to each other, on their behalf.

And then, less than two weeks before Laura's fortieth birthday, Patrick had a fatal heart attack while playing golf. He died in the ambulance, as Laura raced to reach him.

When she rang a few days later, her voice faltered over the funeral arrangements.

"Is there anything I can do?" I asked.

"Not really..." She hesitated, and then went on: "Actually, there is something. Could you help me clear out his room?"

"What, already?" I couldn't hide my shock and it made her angry.

"Of course, already! It's like a morgue in there. I'm not living with that! And I'm not turning it into a shrine, either!" She gave a familiar snort of derision. "So, will you come or not?"

"Yes...yes, I will. When were you thinking?"

That same afternoon, it turned out. She'd sold his desk on Gumtree and the buyer was coming round after work to collect it.

It was a flat-top, kneehole desk, with three stack drawers on one side and a cupboard on the other. As we knelt on the carpet sorting through their contents, I fished out a box file from the bottom of the cupboard. I could feel loose things moving inside and I handed it to her.

She opened the grey, marbled cover. An envelope, with *Laura* written in the middle of it, lay on top of what looked like a dictionary.

"Idiot!" she said, tearing it open. She extracted a playful card and flipped it open. Beneath the printed 'Happy 40th Birthday', in

Patrick's handsome, copperplate italics, was the message: "Wishing you a most rambunctious celebration!"

"Oh, you're impossible!" she fumed at his signature, struggling to suppress her smile.

Overcome by the poignancy of her hidden affection, I seized the dictionary, pretending to look up the 'r' word. Instead, inside I found a neat square cut out in the centre of the pages and a small black box nestled there.

As I held the open dictionary towards her; alarm flickered in her eyes and her fingers trembled pushing up the box's lid. There, cushioned on velvet, lay an elegant brooch of crossed duelling pistols, their barrels silver and their stocks of white gold, each finely initialled, one with a ruby *L* and the other an emerald *P*.

"I'll get you for this, Patrick Dillon!" she said, pinning it to her sweater.

Okay, Shoot!

*by **Charles Becker***

A young cowboy sneaks up, gun drawn, on an old cowboy, whose pulling on his breeches by a campfire.

YC: Get your hands up!

OC: If I put my hands up, my pants gonna fall down.

YC: Okay, fix your braces, but no tricks. I'm longin' to shoot ya.

OC: What I done to you, young fella?

YC: They say you been seein' my girl.

OC: Musta been a clear day. (*Old cowboy takes off his glasses and polishes them*)

YC: You think I'm foolin'?

OC: No, not foolin'. Foolish, maybe. No young woman gonna look at me, not the way you mean.

YC: That's not what I heard. Heard you got a sweet talking way with you.

OC: Why don't ya seat yourself and I'll pour us some coffee?

YC: Don't move, Mister, or I'll cut you down!
(They stand in silence facing each other)

OC: What we gonna do now?

YC: Bartender, in Abilene, told me you and Dixie been dancin' all night through. Real close, he said.

OC: She your girl?

YC: Fianced, ain't we? Getting married in the fall.

OC: Fianced? What's that mean?

YC: Means we're promised to one another. Means I'm gonna shoot your nuts off for messin' with her!

OC: Bartender not tell ya Dixie's my niece?

YC: Yeah, sure! You're her uncle and I'm Wyatt Earp!

OC: Glad to meet you, Marshal. Thought you'd be older by now/...

YC: Funny man, ha? Bet you/...

OC: Thought a big lawman like you woulda had a full-grown moustache, not that lizard's lick slidin' cross the top o' your lip.

YC: Any time you want to try me, old man. Just make your move.
(Silence)

OC: I'm only sweet-talkin' ya, son. No need to get all riled up
over nothin'.

YC: Dixie ain't nothin'! You act like you think she is, you gonna
end up with your hands folded. Know what I mean?

OC: Seems like you need to go see Dixie 'bout me, set your
mind at rest.

YC: You her uncle, tell me what her mama's called.

OC: Belle and me, we grew up in Tulsa. That was her name
then. Don't know what she's using now. Haven't seen her in
a while.

YC: Lies always gonna find you out, mister. I knew you was a
liar. Dixie's mama died givin' birth to her.

OC: Yessir, she did, God rest her soul. But her pa couldn't cope
with a littl'un and took hisself another wife. That was my
sister, Belle, and she was the only mother Dixie ever knew.
Always did call her 'Ma'.

YC: You're twistin' and turnin' like a sidewinder. And I don't give
snakes no second chance. I always shoot 'em.

OC: Hold on a dang minute there and don't go spittin' in your
beans! I've got somethin' here gonna show you got nothin'
to worry about.
(*OC puts his hand in his trouser pocket*)

YC: Real slow or you're vulture meat!
(*OC slowly withdraws a smart phone from his pocket and
starts thumbing the screen; then, he holds it out towards YC,
pointing with his finger*)

OC: That's Dixie on her third birthday; there's her Pa and that's
Belle; and there's me helpin' her cut the cake. Good lookin'
fella back then, weren't I?

YC: Looks pretty sharp, old timer. How many megapixels you
got?
(*YC whips a smart phone from a clip on his gun belt*)
Mine's got 5 mp.

OC: You got me beat there, son. Tell you what; let me move

23

round here some, so the sun's behind yer. Right, hold on a second, and then you can take a picture o' me to give to Dixie.

(*OC takes off his hat and smoothes his hair back. Then, he licks his finger tips and strokes his moustache and eyebrows outwards. Finally, he swells his chest and gives a big smile*)

Okay, shoot!

ITALIAN PROMISES

by *Julie Birkett*

Eddie paused to catch his breath before continuing his climb up the steep hill. He had forgotten just how steep the roads were around here. It was a long time since he had been here, must be fifty years. Could it really have been so long? He paused, his breathing laboured. Must be the heat, he thought. Either that or he was getting old. Silly old fool; of course he was getting old, wasn't that why he was here?

He set off again, if memory serves me right he thought the village should be just around the next bend. There it was just as he remembered it.

The village shimmered in the heat it's stones bleached by the sun. He shaded his eyes, with a hand that shook slightly. Now that he was actually here he was at a loss of what to do next. He could hardly go barging in after all these years. It had been too long. He had promised to come back, and he had fully intended to keep his promise. What was he going to do now go marching in?

'Sorry I couldn't make it sooner, better late than never'

After all he was only fifty years late. What excuse could he offer?

'Sorry life got in the way'

He walked into the village square. Close up he could see that things had changed. Several of the houses looked empty, and the Barbour shop on the corner was no longer there. The café however was, and judging by the tables spilling out over the pavement and the tubs of bright red geraniums it was open for business.

'Just what I need' he said to himself 'A long cool drink while I work out what to do next'

Who was he kidding, what he should do next was turn and walk back down the hill, he should never have come. Fancy thinking that she would still be here after all this time, and what if she was. She certainly wouldn't want to see some old man who once many years ago had held her hand, kissed her lips and promised her the world.

25

He had been young and handsome then, in his Army uniform. Cap in hand he had made his promises and left never to return, until now that is.

'Too late' he muttered shaking his head.

How had it happened? Why did he listen to them?

'What do you want to marry a foreigner for?' his friends had said 'Plenty of nice English girls right here'

'Don't want no funny foreigner in this family' said his father.

'She will only be able to cook that foreign muck' said his mother In the end it had been easier, safer to listen.

He had never forgotten her, his Gabriela. He kept the memories safely hidden away to be pulled out when he was alone. They sustained him when life was tough, the thought of another life waiting for him. Sometimes when things were good she lay forgotten for months at a time, until the smell of evening jasmine reminded him of warm Italian evenings. Or the taste of sun ripe tomatoes conjured up the taste of pasta shared with cheap wine and laughter.

There leading off the square was the street where she had lived above the local bakers; Her father a short round man always covered in a fine dusting of flour, her mother pressing a bag of warm pastries in his hands as he left, football with her brother and his friends. Memories threatened to engulf him. He turned away from the street entrance. Get a drink first he thought, sit down in the shade. He felt in his pocket for his wallet.

'Dam.' He said out loud.

His pocket was empty, his wallet in his jacket still in the car. The car parked at the bottom of the hill. He had wanted to approach on foot like he used to. He dug deep in his pocket and brought out a handful of change, should be enough he thought turning once more towards the café.

He frowned the tables seemed to be moving. The chairs were moving as well. In fact everything was moving. He knew what he was seeing but his brain failed to make any sense out of it. He lurched unsteadily as the ground beneath him bucked and groaned. He put his hand out to steady himself feeling the weathered stone of the wall vibrate under his fingers. A glass fell from one of the tables and smashed loudly to the ground. The bright red geraniums nodded their heads in some wild manic dance. A long low primeval groan rose around him, still he did not understand what was happening. The noise grew until finally the earthquake erupted in full force. The wall that Eddie was leaning against buckled and cracked he fell with it the stones crowding around him. His last thought was of Gabriella as the dust filled his nostrils and darkness descended.

He awoke in the hospital. He was in a side ward. Outside the open door he could see nurses briskly walking past intent on their duties. Eventually one of them notice he was awake and came in. She spoke to him but the words that came out of her mouth made no sense. He looked at her as if she had gone mad. The nurse picked up his wrist and took his pulse. She shoved a thermometer in his ear, picked up a chart from the bottom of the bed and wrote down her findings. Then saying something unintelligible left the room. He closed his eyes hoping that when he opened them again the world would have righted itself.

The next time he woke there was a man in a white coat standing by the bed reading a chart. He nodded and smiled. It was dark outside. He had no idea how much time had passed. No idea where he was or why, He was too tired to try and figure it out.

It was daylight. There was a pretty young girl smoothing down the sheets pulling them tight across his chest. Seeing that he was awake she poured him a glass of water and supporting him helped him drink it. He couldn't understand a word she said'

'Where am I?' he asked

'Ahh' she nodded 'English that explains a lot'.'

'Who are you and why is everyone speaking rubbish'

He struggled against the restricting bed sheets fighting them and rising panic.

'It's OK' she said in her best English pushing him back against the pillows. 'Your in hospital, there was an earthquake, don't you remember?'

'Earthquake' he repeated stupidly 'what are you talking about, how long have I been here, where is here?'

'It's ok calm down, just tell me what you remember'
So he thought and found that he could remember very little. So little in fact that he couldn't remember where he was or even who he was.

The days that followed passed in a blur. There was a succession of doctors pulling and prodding, tests and scans for everything imaginable. Eventually John, as he had been named by the staff, well they had to call him something and John Doe was the name written on his notes. John Doe was pronounced fit and well, considering that is, he had survived an earthquake and had no recollection of who he was or where he had come from.

The earthquake he learned was not a major one and they were used to them in this part of the world. He had been far enough from the epicentre to escape serious injury. Just a few cuts and bruises and of course concussion resulting in his loss of memory. They said it would come back in time but he wasn't so sure.

John looked forward to seeing the young nurse, she was something familiar in an unfamiliar world, where there were no points of reference. It was as if he had begun his existence in this world as an old man, he didn't even know how old he was.
'Hello John how are you feeling today' she peered around the door
'Come in' he waved at the chair beside his bed 'come and talk to me'
'Have you remembered anything yet?'
John shook his head.
'Tell me about yourself, tell me about your life as I can't remember anything about mine. I don't even know your name, and you've been kind enough to visit me every day.'
'Gabby' she said sitting herself down
'That's a pretty name short for...'
'Gabriella after my grandmother'
'And tell me Gabby where do you live and why is such a pretty girl hiding herself away working in a hospital when she should be on stage or in the films?'
Gabby laughed

28

'And there was me thinking only Italian men knew how to charm a girl. Well I live in town, but most of my family live in the village up on the hill. You know the one where they found you. Are you sure you can't remember what you were doing there?'

John shook his head

'I wish I could. I don't know what I was doing in Italy in the first place let alone why I was up in the village. Do you think someone is missing me, looking for me?'

'I'm sure you have family somewhere' she said patting his hand.

'Maybe they are in England and don't expect you back yet'

'Or maybe there is no one' He sighed

The next morning Gabby came bounding into the room.

'I have so many things to tell you I don't know where to start.'

She held out a brown paper bag

'What's this'

'Something to cheer you up, for your breakfast' she said as he pulled out a large buttery croissant. 'Freshly baked this morning by my uncle up in the village.'

'Well tell him from me it's the best croissant I've ever tasted.' He mumbled through a mouthful of pastry. 'At least I think it's the best I really can't remember any others.'

'Well he's had lots of practice, everyone in the family has worked in the bakery at some time or another for as long as I can remember. My mother helped out right up until I was born, even my grandmother worked there for a time after my grandfather was lost in the war.'

'Lost?'

'Yes. She always said lost, as if he was a set of keys that would someday turn up.'

'May be he will, perhaps he was injured and lost his memory like me. He might turn up someday.'

' I doubt it after all this time. Why would he have left her to bring up a baby on her own if he could have come back? Anyway I have other news for you. They've found you car''

'What?' he said staring at her

'A car, it's a hire car, found it buried under a collapsed wall at the bottom of the hill, must be yours, who else around here would hire

29

a car. It's not as if we get a lot of tourists. It must be yours. Oh John we can find out who you are at last.' She paused for breath ' 'I'll let you know as soon as there is ant more news'

She disappeared out the door. John finished his croissant. He wasn't sure he wanted to know who he was. What if he was running away from something? Why else would he have been here in that small Italian village, what was he hiding from? What was he looking for? He wasn't sure he wanted to know.

'Edward, Edward Harper. That's your name' Said Gabby sometime later ' The police traced it to a hire company at the airport.'

'Edward' John said

It sounded odd, not at all familiar the name of a stranger.

It was later that day that John found out that he was Edward Harper from Essex. He was a widower and had one daughter, Veronica. He spoke to her that evening on the telephone. He had no recollection of her, her voice sounded very English after the Italian accents he was used to. It was agreed she would come and collect him as soon as she could get a flight. She wanted to know why he was there, what he was doing Italy. Why had he gone off without telling anybody, but john had no answers for her.

So it was his last morning Veronica was due in a few hours. Come to take him home, home to somewhere he didn't know and wasn't sure he wanted to go to.

'All set Edward?' asked Gabby

'I wish you wouldn't call me that' He grumbled

'Why ever not,' she exclaimed 'It's your name.'

'But I've got used to John now'

'Come on, everything will be fine. You might even remember something when you see Veronica, after all she is your daughter'

'I wish you were my daughter' he blurted out

She looked at him indignantly.

'Well all right granddaughter'

'That's more like it' she laughed as she handed over a white cardboard box. 'Something special for you to take home with you.'

Inside was a huge Panettone glistening and studded with sugar.

'You can share it with your daughter and remember us.'

30

She kissed him on both cheeks Italian style.
'You take care now Edward and when you're fit and well again I want you to come back and meet all my family and perhaps we can work out why you were here.'
'I will Gabriella' he said using her full name for the first time.
'Promise now, promise me you will come back.'
'I will, I promise Gabriella.'

The Keeper of Secrets

*by **Julie Birkett***

It was grandfather that taught me about Lynx Magic, that turned out not to be magic at all.

I must have been about five or six when I wandered off as young boys do. Unknown to me my mother had been frantic, searching everywhere for me. She should have gone straight to Grandfather, he always knew where everything was, even those things that no one else could find. She had given up all hope of finding me, thinking I had been carried off by a wolf, or drowned in the river. Grandfather led her through the forest until they came to a clearing. There I was sitting in the middle, surrounded by sunlight and grass staring at the lynx. Mother went to rush in and save me, but Grandfather stopped her. Everything, everybody was still. A picture frozen in the sunlight. The big cat looked at me and I stared back at him. His black ear tufts quivered and he slowly blinked. Standing he slowly stretched dipping his front legs muscles rippling like water beneath his golden coat. He padded over to me. There was a sharp intake of breath from mother. Grandfather laid a restraining hand on her arm. The Lynx sniffed my hair. I smiled up at him. Close up I could see thick fur glinting in the sun, his breath warm and meaty on my cheek. Turning he looked at Grandfather, something passed between them. Grandfather nodded once. The lynx turned and bounded off disappearing into the forest like a whisp of smoke. Things changed after that.

The next day grandfather took me back to the clearing. He told me to sit there and watch and observe and he would be back soon. At first I thought that the lynx might come back. Then I realised that wasn't going to happen. I grew board but daren't disobey Grandfather.   Eventually he returned and asked me what I had seen,

'Nothing'

'Nothing' He repeated 'What do you mean nothing.'

'There's nothing here but trees and grass, nothing interesting just trees and grass'

He frowned.

'Boy you are looking but not seeing. Stay there until you see'
With that he stomped off. I didn't know what I was supposed to see there really wasn't anything there. A bird flew into the tree, I could see she had a nest there and watched as she flew back and forth insects in her beak feeding her hungry brood. Good I thought that would be something to tell Grandfather. When he returned I told him about the bird.

'What colour was she? How many times did she fly to the nest? How many chicks did she have?'
The questions came thick and fast and I had no answers to them.

'You need to see more boy, you will do better tomorrow.'
And so the rhythm of my day was set. Each day Grandfather would take me to the clearing and tell me to watch, to see, to observe.
Each day I hoped that I would see something, something that would please Grandfather.

As the days went on I began to notice more and more. I watched the bird feeding her growing chicks. Plotting her course as she flew in search of insects. I observed the ants crawling through the grass carrying leaves on their backs. I saw the shiny black beetles and watched as the bird flew down and took them back to the nest. Sometimes Grandfather seemed please with what I had seen and other times not. He told me to listen and to smell. At first it was hard, as it had been hard to see. But each day I could see and hear and smell more and more. Grandfather no longer took me to the clearing I wanted to go to see what had happened, what had changed in my absence. As the seasons changed I watched the clearing changing. The ground grew dry and crumbly baked in the sun, I could hear the insects humming and buzzing. I began to know what insects liked which plants. I watched the fledglings first flight. When the rains came I saw a rainbow reflected in a raindrop that hung trembling from the grass. I learned how long it took for the ground to dry, I could tell by the soil when the rains had last come. I could smell the scent of sweet grass on the warm winds that blew across the grasslands, and feel the chill of the winds that blew down from the snow clad mountains. There was so much to see I couldn't believe that I had once thought that it was boring and there was nothing happening in the clearing.

When winter came and the ground was frozen and the insects had fallen silent, Grandfather would come and place a blanket around my shoulders. Sometimes he would sit beside me and watch with me. I enjoyed his silent company and begged him on the way home to tell me what he had seen in case I had missed something. As I grew older I would sit and observe other places. The river, the forest itself. Each place slowly revealed its secrets to me. I pleaded with mother to let me sit in the clearing at night, she was fearful that the lynx would come back and carry me off, she always said no. I appealed to Grandfather but he said that I must respect my mother and one day I would be old enough to make my own decisions.

When I was ten years old, I was told I would have to go to the white man's school and learn to read and write and become an American. I didn't want to go no one did, but I wasn't old enough yet to make my own decisions. Grandfather said I should go and learn to make the marks on paper and to understand what they meant. He said it was good to know your enemy, to understand their world and learn their weakness. He told me to look and observe as I had done in the clearing. And so I went. The place was filled with hate and fear. There was no grass or insects just a black hearted teacher who beat us for every misdemeanour. Despite this I learned to read and write though I never did learn to become an American.

Eventually mother relented and allowed me to stay out and observe at night. I think Grandfather might have had something to do with this. It was like another world, yet it was the same place. Another dimension bathed in starlight. I watched the stars each night as they moved across the sky. Grandfather taught me their names, and showed me the lynx constellation faintly glowing in the northern sky. I learned their positions and what direction they travelled in. Where they were in the winter and where they were in the summer. I watched the night animals stalking their prey.

As I approached my 12 year and my initiation ceremony that would make me a man, grandfather began to tell me about the lynx.

34

'Remember' he said 'the lynx is the keeper of secrets not the teller of secrets. The knower of that which is secret. The lynx observes and waits in silence and secrets are revealed to him.'

I tried to put this into practice and found that it was true. If I waited and said nothing people rushed to fill the silence and in doing so revealed far more than they knew. Lies were spoken with a downward glance an uncomfortable shift. Expressions and stance speaking the truth while words told lies. The land revealed all its secrets to those that knew how to see and hear them.

On the night of my initiation Tatanka the holy man draped in a buffalo skin sang chanted and danced. Everyone sang and danced the atmosphere was charged with emotion. As the night grew long Grandfather drew me away to the clearing.

'Go into the silence boy' he said 'learn to understand the hidden knowledge and ancient wisdom.'

I knelt down and lifted my face to the stars.

'Lynx of smiling hidden secrets
Bring aid and wisdom to me now
Keeper of ancient secrets
Teacher of hidden skills.'

I chanted and then I was alone.

I began to run through the forest. Leaping and bounding over fallen branches my feet silent over the forest floor. Then there he was running besides me, the moonlight glinting off his eyes, his fur thick and sleek. I matched him stride for stride. Effortlessly we ran, up through the forest higher and higher past the tree line, on to the rocky outcrop higher, yet higher still. We ran together until we became as one. Through the snow clad slopes up and up until we could touch the stars. The blood ran fast as we jumped and leaped with the sheer joy of being alive. We hunted silent and deadly and I tasted blood on my lips. The mountain bright as day awash with starlight. On and on we went until I thought that we would never stop. As daylight dawned the sun low and red in the sky I made my way down the mountain and back to the village. Mother and Grandfather were waiting, I had been gone a week.

Much time has passed since that night and I have run with the Lynx on many occasions, but none compare to that first time. I am old now and spend my time sitting on the porch, still I watch still I see. I have watched as my people slowly die. The white man's germs have killed our bodies and the white man's lies have killed our spirit. Grandfather was right it was useful to know how to read and write. I could read the treaties the false promises of land and I could write letters of protest to the American government as we were all Americans now. But he was wrong that knowing your enemy would be our strength. We could not fight them they killed our Buffalo until none remain, without them we could not survive. We were weak and starving, smiling they offered food and shelter in exchange for our lands. How can one man own land? The land is for all to use to support all men and all animals. The land is for everyone to take from as they need no more no less, no one owns the land. Our people have started to forget who they are. They have lost themselves in the bottom of a whisky bottle. Still a memory lives within them. In their dreams they know they hold the power to heal their bodies and soles. To bring the rains when needed they know they can find their place in the natural world again.

Who will come after me when I am gone who will be the Keeper of Secrets. No one has learned to see, to listen, to smell. No one will observe the changing of the seasons and the passing of the years. I am the last of my line, no one knows my secrets.

The lynx is there standing on the barren earth in front of my porch. He waits. I shrug off the blanket around my shoulders and slowly rise my stiff joints shrieking in protest. I descend the steps, I draw closer to the magnificent big cat. His ear tufts tremble in anticipation. We walk to the edge of the forest together each step easier than the last. I turn and take one last look at the old man on the porch. Then together we are running through the forest. The blood running fast as we leap and bound, higher and higher we go until as one we can touch the stars.

Good Things Ahead

*by **Mary Curd***

The white envelope fluttered down to the carpet. Anne glanced at the closed door of the spare room, expelled relief in a deep breath, and looked up at the open window in front of her. 'Must be the draught from there,' she thought.

The envelope looked commonplace enough, marked "private and confidential", but the four-letter code in the corner had alerted her. She should have hidden it away. Instead, she had been daydreaming, peeling away the past in onion skin layers and imagining different outcomes. She touched the sticky open flap and felt, kneaded, the single sheet of notepaper within.

'Anne! Are you ready?' George's shout was followed by the sound of the dog's frantic scraping of paws from the stone-flagged porch.

'Coming, George. Just give me a minute!' Anne thrust the letter deep into a jumble of old papers at the bottom of the chest of drawers.

The dog's excited yelps turned into imperative short barks as Anne stepped into the hall. She bent to stroke Danny as his warm lolling tongue reached her hand. She attached the dog's collar as George leaned heavily on his walking stick.

George had made so much progress since the stroke, but with all the optimism in the world – he was still in his early fifties – there was no knowing what further improvement he could hope for. Yet she had been able to return to work part-time and George was becoming more independent. Sometimes, when she returned home, she found the house empty and a note left to say he had gone to the fitness centre which catered for his needs, or that he was visiting former colleagues.

His physical weakness upset him, but today he seemed to look at *her* with compassion, and the tenderness she saw inspired

37

pathos. She took his free arm by the elbow and he accepted her support with a smile.

It was quiet as they walked through the woods. No planes cut through the sky above the canopy of trees. Danny was far ahead, pausing to snuffle now and then amongst the musty, wet leaves. As they trudged along, she picked out all the colours; pallid greens, yellows blotted with red, and others which had turned into a wrinkled crisp brown. They were lucky to live here, away from the noise and pressure of the city.

'What were you thinking about just now? George asked.

'When we first met. How kind you were, rescuing me from that life.'

They paused under a tree. George looked upward for the source of the birdsong, a repetitive complicated trill. 'You were a bit mixed up, pregnant and everything, too, that's all. And it was the times, then. Anyway, you were a lovely young girl. Still are.' He smoothed a thick tress of Anne's hair and pulled it forward over her shoulder. 'Don't look back,' he said, 'there will be good things ahead. You've been through a lot. What with me and all this.' He raked his walking stick along the ground, scattering a pile of brittle leaves, raising a fine dust which hovered and slowly dispersed. 'Anyway, I wasn't always kind to you in those days.'

'I still don't know what you saw in me when we first met. Taking all kinds of drugs, living in that hostel and ...'

They had been over this so many times but the letter had prompted her reflections again today. She knew that she was only hoping for reassurance from him.

'We fell in love. That's simple enough. They say that love conquers all.' George laughed, stopped abruptly, and clutched her hand.

Two weeks later, Anne took the letter out of her handbag and read it again. The single, crumpled sheet had been with her everywhere after that day when she had secreted it away in the drawer in the spare room. She had to make up her mind about it. Once, she had crushed it for good, and thrown it into the waste-paper basket in the office at work, only to immediately retrieve it. She told herself that it was too incriminating to dispose of so casually where any prying or curious eye might see it and pick it out. But she knew it was a lie to cover her indecision.

She pictured the photograph; she never carried it with her and had stopped looking at it long ago. The image was a part of her now; burnt into her brain. Obsessed with looking at it, she had tried to fathom from the expression in the eyes, the soft smile, what thoughts lay behind the face. It ended in nothing but fruitless, spiralling supposition.

This was her last chance. The agency informed her that if she did not contact them by the end of the month, communication would cease, as she had previously requested.

Still Anne hesitated, roaming in her head over all the old questions. Could her married life really have been different? If they had had a child together, everything might have worked out. And when it became obvious there was a difficulty because she did not conceive, she had thought there were treatments for that, weren't there? Even though it was probably all her own fault and a consequence of her wild early life.

In the end though, it was George's infertility, not hers.

'A cruel twist of fate,' a friend had tried to comfort her. After that Anne had worked hard to build a career in textile design to carry her forward and wipe out the past. It was creative work which she loved and it had periodically enabled her to travel across Europe.

George had confessed in the end. To make her feel better, perhaps. Or the guilt was too hard to contain any longer. He had urged her to sign the child away. The baby's responses didn't look right to him. All the things she had done, her drug habit and lifestyle in those teenage years, what on earth might they portend? He had lied.

Anne plucked a tissue from the box on her office desk. George had said that good things lay ahead. Maybe she should lay some ghosts to rest. She picked up the phone.

The sunshine lifted her spirits, but did nothing for her nerves. Anne slowed her pace as she neared the Bistro. She had checked her watch so many times and now she was a bit too early. Panic fluttered in her throat and stomach. It seemed important all of a sudden that she had never answered any of the personal letters. The communications had all been one-way, except that final arrangement with the agency.

Anne knew exactly which face to look for as she plunged through the door with her last scrap of resolve, and she found it within a few beats of her racing heart. But as she approached the nook, low-lit and furnished with a coffee table bordered by two sofas, she saw someone else sitting there as well.

'George! What on earth …?'

'Sit down, Anne. We've got you a drink,' said George.

'It's OK. Everything's fine. George and I have already met.'

Finally, Anne heard her daughter's voice. Rich and with the trace of an accent. Northern? Anne sank down heavily on the sofa, fanning her face, the breath knocked out of her.

'Her hair is not the same as in the photo,' Anne thought. 'It's shorter – very pretty.'

'You must take a few minutes. We both should. It's a shock, isn't it? George will explain how we met,' her daughter said, turning towards George. They looked at each other with affectionate, smiling eyes.

Anne felt anger and resentment boiling up as she thought, 'You could have loved her, George, you fool! Look how she's turned out!' She clamped down hard on the destructive emotions. They would do no good. If this was a second chance, she must not waste it.

George was speaking but she could not take it in. She caught only phrases: 'found Susie's letters, and the agency's; when I was staying in the spare room, after the stroke … not sleeping well then.'

He was telling her about how strict the agency had been and trying to justify this intrusion. No exchange of information had been allowed, nor names and addresses. But he had established his identity as Anne's husband, and they had passed on his message to her daughter.

Susie joined in now. He called her 'Susie'. Her daughter's name, uttered by him.

40

'George told me about your difficult circumstances, Anne. You were very young, I knew that. Susie leaned forward across the table, 'And what he made you do. He regrets that so much.'

Their faces blurred. Anne put out a trembling hand for her drink and felt George's cover hers, stilling it. Then the pressure of another hand on top of his.

'Were you … happy? I need to know! Was it all right?' Anne asked.

Susie's voice, tender and warm, 'I was only a baby and much too young to be aware of loss, Anne. My parents didn't tell me that I was adopted until I was sixteen. The law had changed and they wanted to give me the choice of finding my birth mother. If I wanted to.'

Susie sat back. Smiled. 'I have children, Anne. A boy and a girl. Leo and Millie. Your grandchildren. I hope you will come to meet them,' she said.

George shifted in his seat and caught his toppling walking stick. He stood up and awkwardly made his way around to Anne in the limited space. With an arm on her shoulder, pulling her close, he said, 'I did try to tell you, my love, that there would be good things ahead.'

'Are there, George?' she thought. She remembered all those years ago when they had been childless for so long, and George had finally confessed to her that he could never have accepted another man's child. All those false, oh so reasonable excuses, when she had given birth to her daughter, 'Another home, a "neutral" family, would give her the best chance in life,' he had said at the time. But he had admitted, at last, the real reason. 'I could never have loved her. Not another man's child.'

Anne looked at her daughter's face, so familiar from the photograph. 'We are strangers,' she thought. 'How can anyone repair all those lost years?'

'There's Leo and Millie growing up fast now,' Susie said, almost as if she had heard Anne speak aloud. 'We can all enjoy that, can't we?'

NAOMI

by *John Curry*

I'm glad that's over. When you get to my age you start to go to
funerals more often than weddings and christenings. This is the
third cremation this month. I'm starting to be quite a connoisseur.
The big giveaway is the rent-a-vicar. So few people go to church
these days, the chances of the vicar ever having actually met the
dear departed is getting very slim. Still, the family want things done
properly. "We've always been C of E." they say. That stands for
Church of Expedience I think.

It was a lady vicar today, still seems odd that, but she did very
well. Nice singing voice too, not shy, trilling her way through 'The
Lord is my Shepherd' while the congregation of about two dozen
were muttering and groaning, dragged along by the organist.

The dear departed this time was Mrs Cox, used to be a near
neighbour of ours before she lost her marbles and went to live in a
home. I used to visit every so often. She had a son, Brian, he lives
up North, somewhere near Halifax so he wasn't around much. I
saw him when he came down to sell the house and deal with all her
stuff. You see this brooch? That was hers. Brian asked me to
choose something to remember her by. It's nice isn't it? Brian said
he'd decided on a cremation so there wouldn't be a grave to
maintain. Just scatter the ashes and get on with life.

That wouldn't have been right for Mum. She wanted to be buried
"proper like". She hardly weighed anything at the end. I know
because I helped carry her. "Are you sure?" said the chief
undertaker. I gave him one of my looks. End of discussion. I had
thought about keeping her wedding ring, well I would have if she'd
been cremated. I wouldn't put it past them blokes at the crem to
rake through the ashes. I bet that's one of their perks. No, that
stayed on her finger where it belonged.

I've got used to being on my own. I say I've got used to it, which
is not the same as liking it. I don't think I was designed to be on my
own. If you'd asked me thirty years ago what I thought my future

would be I'd have said married to Ian Bettinson with a couple of kids. It was just after Ian and I got married that Mum got ill. Dad had already died in an accident at work. It was a terrible time. His firm were found guilty of negligence and were fined a lot of money. Mum had a big payout as well as his pension so we were never pushed financially, but if all that weren't enough Mum got the cancer in her spine.

It was probably a mistake, but Ian and I started our married life living with Mum. It made sense at the time. I could keep my eye on Mum, who refused to take any rent off us, so we could save up for a deposit. We both worked and pretty soon, after about a year and a half we had enough saved and we started looking for somewhere to buy. That's when the trouble started.

Ian would come home from work with Estate Agents' details of local properties within our price range. Ones we thought looked OK we'd arrange to go and see. Then one day he came home all excited. He'd heard from someone he worked with about a detached house in Burden. Now Burden is about fifteen miles away and suddenly I realised, and I could see it in his eyes that Ian realised it too, that I didn't want to leave my Mum on her own.

Poor Ian. He tried, God bless him, he did try to come to terms with the feeling of being second best. We talked endlessly into the early hours over the next few months. He loved me and never once gave me the classic ultimatum: "Your mum or me". But in the end he applied for a job three hundred miles away and got it. I said I'd follow him when I could.

Mum was devastated when Ian left. And she'd guessed what was behind the move. She told me time and time again to go after him. But I couldn't. We'd end up in tears of sadness and frustration.

To begin with we were in touch every day, then once a week, then came the letter. He couldn't go on like that any longer. He thought it best to break the contact. He'd decided he wanted to go travelling. I could read the tears between the lines. So that was that. I can't say I blamed him. I didn't, I don't. Gradually the hurt grew less and although he was never far from my thoughts, I simply learnt how to become a different me.

Some time after Mum's funeral I thought I'd try to contact Ian again. I really don't know what I was thinking. Did I really expect he'd come running? No, of course not. Most of me hoped that he'd forgotten all about me and found someone else to be happy with. I got a brief note back from the last address I had for him. They'd no idea where he was. They'd had a postcard from Spain just after he'd left but that was it.

I got fed up living on my own in that big house, so I sold it to a nice young couple with two kids and another on the way. They needed more room. I found a lovely two-bedroom ground floor flat with a good sized garden. I've been there ever since. I like it. With the profit from the sale and what money Mum left me I had enough to take early retirement. I do a bit of voluntary work in a couple of charity shops and there's a tea dance every month in the village hall. I read a lot.

As it happens I did hear about Ian a couple of weeks ago. About him not from him. I got a letter and a parcel from Spain. Someone called Tony Bishop who'd got to know Ian quite well. The letter explained that Ian had settled in southern Spain, he ran small bar, lots of ex-pats as well as locals. Before he died Ian gave Tony some instructions on what he wanted. It was all arranged and paid for. Ian wanted to be buried here in St. Michael's. So I'll be back here again next week. Tony also sent me a parcel of letters that Ian wrote to me over the years but never posted. They're in this bag here with his wedding ring. As I say, I read a lot.

LEATHER ON WILLOW

*by **John Curry***

A cricket ball is a time machine. A cherry red comet streaking back through time, leaving a glowing trail of memories in white. Five and a half ounces of cork, string and leather, dyed and lacquered into a sphere of jewel-like beauty. Toss it from hand to hand and feel the six equatorial rows of stitching inviting you to spread your fingers around it and grasp its potential. To do so instantly transports you back to past glories and miseries which, Kiplingesque, have made you what you have become.

The cheer from the middle is curiously echoed by a groan from those around me in the pavilion. It is my first game, in the second eleven, with the men. Someone reminded me, unnecessarily, that I was 'in'. I was number eleven, last man in. I needed to survive one over for the match to be drawn. Defend my precious wicket for only six balls to become a hero. I stood up and checked my pads were secure. I was fifteen, slightly built, just over five feet tall, with National Health glasses, which, if the word had been around at the time, would announce the imminent arrival at the wicket of a nerd. I self consciously, adjusted my box. I remember the day I bought it. It resembled nothing so much as a bright pink soap dish. I recall the apprehension I felt going into the local sports shop to buy it. Actually it was not the soap dish that worried me, it was the question I was anticipating concerning what size jock-strap did I want? Small, medium or large were the options. With consummate comic timing the shop keeper paused to enjoy my embarrassment before adding one's waist size was the key statistic required.

I waddled across the greensward with all the elegance of a baby penguin and arrived at the wicket a little out of breath. My bat was slightly too big for me, but it was the smallest one available in the club kit bag. The batting gloves were my own, a birthday present from my Yorkshire born, and therefore cricket-mad, granddad. On reflection I placed rather too much faith in the protective qualities of the green plastic pimples running along the backs of my fingers.

45

My memory banks are full of images of grandad bowling underarm leg breaks with a tennis ball on the unforgiving wicket of the path which ran along the front of their cottage. Playing straight and along the ground were essential. On the leg side were the cottage windows of Miss Russell and Mrs Cox. On the off-side were cabbages, lettuces and chrysanthemums in grandad's garden. Although a kind and generous man, he seldom saw the funny side of potential prize-winning blooms being decapitated by a square cut, however well executed.

I took my guard from the umpire. Middle and leg, as advised by my first cricketing mentor. Even to this day I've never had a discussion about choice of guard. All through my cricketing life I took the same guard, not through well-thought out tactical thinking but more through superstition. I never wanted to tempt the cricketing Gods by going against sacred tradition.

The final ritual before settling down to facing my first ball was to cast an eye round to take note of the disposition of the fielders. The reasoning here being to enable the batsman to cunningly place scoring shots out of the reach of said fielders. Or indeed where it could be safe to loft the ball tantalisingly over and just beyond their grasping fingers. In this particular instance however, the outfield was essentially deserted, the opposing skipper had brought all his personnel within touching and, more importantly, close catching distance, reasoning quite correctly that I was unlikely to risk such adventure, even if capable of doing so.

I settled at the crease to await the first delivery, the umpire turned to nod to the bowler who had been pacing around at the end of his run like a Spanish bull scenting a matador and not disguising his impatience to do some damage. I sighted the first ball quickly and judged line and length instinctively and more importantly, accurately. The ball started to swing to the off side a little as it left the hand. Early and therefore predictable. I adjusted to anticipate the point where the ball would pitch. Somewhere in my brain my grandad's advice was being processed at lightning speed. Left elbow up, show him the maker's name, good stride forward to the pitch, head over and in line, smell the leather.

Smack! The ball hit the middle of my bat and rolled back the way it had come. The eleven fielders surrounding me like a white picket fence exhaled loudly and stood up, shaking the tension from their limbs.

'Well played lad,' said a voice from one of them.

Quite soon we all settled back and prepared for the next delivery. The bowler, who at this point had been expecting to hear a chorus of congratulation following the noisy clatter announcing the the destruction of my wicket, could hardly contain his impatience.

Smack! The next delivery was a virtual replay of the first.

Smack! The third ball seemed to arrive earlier than the others, the bowler had, as they say, really put his back into it. My hands felt its power despite the springs in the bat handle. I had acquired a little confidence by this time and felt able to look around a bit. Several weather beaten faces looked back at me. They were smiling! One chap clapped silently and winked at me.

The fourth delivery was more problematic. As far as I was concerned I did nothing differently, but this time there was no satisfying thwack of leather on willow. There was a flurry of bat and gloves, pads and boots. The ball had gone straight through, probably I had misjudged the pace. As soon as I realised I had missed it I knew I would hear the death rattle. But no. Eleven pairs of arms shot up with an accompaniment of oohs and aahs and sharp intakes of breath.

'Take it easy Geoff,' said the opposition captain. Clearly bowler Geoff was getting annoyed that this oik at the far end was not giving in easily, and had upped his pace even more.

'Well played lad,' came again.

I realised that the opposition wanted me to succeed, even though that would mean the match, which on the run of play they should have won, would be drawn.

The fifth ball was wide enough outside the off stump for me to allow it to go harmlessly by.

The final ball of the match I blocked with confidence. I turned to walk off back to the pavilion alongside the non-striking batsman.

'He didn't like that, did he? He once had a trial for Northants you know, so he's a bit useful. No he didn't like that at all,' said my team-mate with a grin.

We were caught up by the visiting captain. 'Well played young man. I thought we'd won that but, the way you played Geoff in that last over deserved a draw. Don't expect him to come and shake your hand though, he's not a great loser.'

He was right, though I think everybody else did. I felt proud of myself that day and there have been many days over the years when cricket has given me the chance to feel good about myself. I was, and internally at least still am, a cricketer. We enjoy the competition, but we value at least as much, the love of the spirit of the game.

When from time to time I come across the cricket ball I keep in a drawer, I travel back in time to the day I first realised I could make it swing when I bowled it. Back to the day when we were playing on a park pitch with no marked boundaries. I cut a ball to the off-side cleaner than ever before or since. It disappeared into the distance and we could have run eight but stopped at five out of breath and laughing. Back to the day when practising in the indoor nets I timed an off drive so perfectly that when it hit the wall at the far end halfway up and still rising, it made a sound like a clap of thunder . Back to the day when, still a nerd, I threw the ball in from the edge of the boundary right to the top of the bails to run someone out. The look of disbelief on the batsman's face was priceless. But he was a cricketer, so he looked at me and shouted 'Well thrown lad!' as he walked off to the pavilion.

THICKER THAN WATER

by *John Curry*

You don't need me to tell you what a ghastly thing dementia is, not so much for the victim perhaps for whom it may represent an escape once it has tightened its grip, but for the family, lovers and friends who offer hands to hold and smiles to comfort. My Mum died last year, surrounded in her bed at the nursing home by all those who were dearest to her, but whom she had long ceased to recognise. Dad was sad of course, but not bereft, after all he had begun the grieving process months before, the first time he had visited her to be greeted by the words he had dreaded to hear. "Who are you?"

They had met during the organised chaos that was Dunkirk. He, Ted, had been wounded, shrapnel in his thigh from a mortar explosion. His senses were just returning when he became simultaneously aware of the intense pain and the gentle hands and words of comfort from the young French woman kneeling beside him. He had tried to get up but was firmly pressed back to the ground.

'It is necessare that you move not, m'sieu. I must stop the blood. I am nurse.'

Ted was happy to comply. Despite the lingering odour of cordite, he could detect a delicate floral scent every time she leaned towards him binding the wound with bandages that had been scavenged from the first aid kit in his knapsack.

In later years the story would become increasingly romanticised. The nurse, Madeleine, later to be my mum, helped Ted to reach Dunkirk, and because of her skills was allowed to board a ship and accompany wounded soldiers back to England. She regularly visited Ted in hospital where they had fallen in love. They decided not to marry until the war was over. Madeleine wanted her parents to be able to come, and for the moment they were trapped in France. Once Ted had recovered from his injuries he was sent off

49

to a camp in Wales to train new recruits. Madeleine stayed in London. They wrote to each other every week.

Some time after my Dad died, my sister Judy and I met at the now empty house where we had grown up, to sort through our parents' things. Bitter-sweet doesn't begin to describe the experience.

Photos of family outings, everybody smiling at the camera, brought echoing smiles, but a picture of me wrestling Buster, our beloved but long gone Jack Russel brought tears. Mum and Dad's wedding photo. We decided to do the easy stuff first and bundled clothes and shoes into black plastic bags ready for the charity shop. We each chose a couple of pictures and ornaments then packed the rest into boxes. Local charities were booked to collect furniture, crockery and kitchen stuff.

Then the paperwork.

Dad had been very conscientious in keeping details of monetary matters and important certificates. His will was simplicity itself, a couple of modest legacies to favourite charities then the rest to be split between Judy and me. All fairly normal, really.

Amongst his things we found an envelope addressed to us. Judy opened the letter and started to read. After a short while tears began to form then roll down her cheeks.

'What is it?' I asked. She just shook her head and dabbed at her face with a tissue. When she had finished I took the letter from her and began to read Dad's familiar neat handwriting.

"What I'm telling you now your mum never wanted you to know in case it made you think badly of her, but to me, your mother was the bravest woman I ever knew. As you know, Madeleine was never a nurse, she only pretended to be one to escape from France, always was resourceful, your mum. During the war she was recruited to work in a Government Department where her French was useful. One day she was approached by a man who said he had news of her parents. He said they were fine, but were in danger. He could find out more but he would need a favour first. Obviously Madeleine was suspicious, but he surprised her by being quite open with her. He was a German agent. All she had to do was to meet him perhaps once a month for a cup of tea and he would ask her a few questions. No cloak and dagger stuff, and for that he would use his contacts to ensure her parents' safety. Pure blackmail. He said he would give her a week to think about it.

By the time of their first meeting Madeleine had decided she had to do anything she possibly could to save her parents from being sent to a concentration camp, they were Jewish you see, and she had started to learn about the transportations from her work. She made me promise not to tell you, and perhaps her strong opinions about organised religion now fall into perspective.

So she became a spy.

After the war she discovered that her parents had in fact perished in Auschwitz a week after she had arrived in England.

She told me all this before we married. She thought I deserved to know what sort of person she was marrying. The irony was that I already knew. Madeleine was not a very good spy, and our intelligence service had already identified the agent. They used me to feed duff information to her to pass on to him. Otherwise they would have arrested her. But I could never tell her that. That was my secret. She lived with her guilt for the rest of her life, as I have with mine. This was the lady whose charity work was legendary, could never do enough to help others.

As you know I kept her ashes. It would be my dearest wish if you, Judy and Ben, would take them with mine and bury them in France, in a small village called Cléry, next to the memorial to her parents."

Everyday Lies

*by **Elaine Dorr***

You look lovely in that dress
I can't help you
This diet is going so well
Sorry, no change
You were marvellous, darling
It's me not you
Everything is fine
You'll have so much in common
I read the book
New improved formula
Me too, I love that show
I've never met her
Next day delivery
Of course I think you can do it

Windows Of The Souls.

by *Louis Fletcher*

The two men sat in fireside chairs on either side of the blazing hearth, onto which a fresh log had been added. It was the home of the older of the two and deserted except for them. Each cradled a glass of port wine as if to fortify himself from the darkness and the storm raging outside. Flames licked and spat, noisily consuming the log. Lightning flashed as the men sipped silently, digesting what had just been said.

It was the older who spoke first - and of himself - telling the younger he had the gift of looking into peoples' souls. He saw people as windows - some were firmly shut and needed to be quietly prized while others were found flung wide open; but he could penetrate them all. The expression, 'He saw through me like a pane of glass' made him smile because that is exactly how it was. No effort or strain - he just could. Inside, the good people had a shining which pulsed and surged to take up their physical shape. This had the effect of creating an outline of light which turned them into a pure, incandescent spectre. He saw good intentions as fire and fine white ash. Fire the comforter, the cleanser, the destroyer; fire the renewer.

The bad people had the hue of darkness and when he looked into their souls he could visualise their evil intentions. Some incubated malevolence and yearned for it to take shape, or having formed it they patiently awaited a triggering onset. Primed for iniquity they just needed opportunity - the right spark - to carry out their dreadful desires. These worst of humankind had caged themselves in a carapace of normality and were accomplished actors who only emerged to encourage others into evil and then slip safely back inside. They were the contagious ones, the users and perverters who controlled others, and their powers stemmed from normalising the abnormal and deceiving people into believing that wrong was right, and that repulsive things were good. Those who are easily led often crave association with people whom they admire, they long to be noticed: and the younger man was greatly admired through his media exposure as a doer of good deeds and supporter of charities. Much work had been done to burnish a persona for him; one of caring for others, especially the poor and the sick. His following on social media was vast, he was a well recognised face on television, and idolised as a self-made man who had become a modern-day philanthropist. That he was in touch with, and understood the problems of, society, had led to his being regarded as a champion of the people.

The log settled into the fire and sent up a shower of sparks, and in the same way the older man settled into - and warmed to - his theme. He explained: those longing to be used belong to a herd that drifts at a functioning level. Society has long tolerated dissolution and weakness, has even encouraged it as being meritorious, and these people have turned self-interest into a virtue. They quickly supported opinions, even the implausible, if posted on social media by commentators that they like - simply because they like that person - and the messenger and not the message is all that matters to them. Easily whipped up, they live their lives in flash-burst moments and are dependent on instant gratification gained on an altar of tinsel and baubles; an extremism has taken shape and a new type of blind loyalty has been borne. Believing that selfish pursuits can cause no harm they act for the moment - for laughs - and blind themselves to the danger of being moulded by celebrities and other false pundits. Desperate for an identity, these fools have become prisoners of a collective insanity. It is a Faustian process and irresistible, and because it fills the world with useful idiots it creates its own camouflage. It is behind this false sparkle that evil advances.

Lightning filled the room with a white light from which the younger man shielded his eyes. The wind hummed tunelessly in the chimney as the log flared that bright, fierce flame: the hungry precursor to its own elimination. Having spoken, the older man now mused but kept his thoughts private. The older man knew that the younger had earlier attempted to look into his soul, had felt the amateurish intrusion which had been easily rebuffed, but gently so as not to alert him to this knowing. In return the older man had looked deeply into the younger man's soul and had found his blackness, had found his hidden secrets and his lies - which were legion - had seen his intentions to draw people to him and form them into his personal tools. The younger man had no interest in people except as resources, as disposable commodities to serve the order of his own liking. His desire was to become political without the need for a mandate; this road had been well trodden by previous dictators. The rule of law was a thin tissue which would not stand in his way and, once power had been seized, the consensus of the majority would be an irrelevance. Outwardly he was kindly, but beneath his skin seethed a violent bully and a jumped-up gangster. A trafficker of drugs, guns, and people, he was building huge capital which had already purchased the support of influential people, including celebrities. The power of bribery had not been lost on him and elements of the media were already in his pay. Understanding the power of spin, he had many opinion formers in his thrall, and had established a platform from which the well-known amongst his followers could extol his virtues. Social media sites had been seeded with trusted stooges who posted under numerous false identities, and who continually sang his praises. Daily, websites were flooded with positive news about him.

The younger man was planning the first ever 'coup by internet.' He was in love with the camera and knew his affections would be repaid - the moment was approaching and he was ready. That many people already thought of the younger man in Messianic terms - that he was recognised for his charisma - all appealed to his enormous ego, and to his mass of disciples. He believed it was not co-incidental that his name was used in the same revered tone reserved for Christ, and his mission was to save the World and cleanse it of those he regarded as sinful and unworthy: his people would adore him as a redeemer, and if others died in the doing it would be a price worth paying. He could count on the support of a number of established politicians, including one senior cabinet minister who would proclaim his suitability to lead when instructed to do so, and control of the government website was part of this politicians remit. Social malcontents he controlled in abundance and a huge pool of angry people had been organised to assist his aims. Men and women whose idea of debate was restricted to brief and caustic utterances on social media. These misfits, drawn from the ranks of the violent and dispossessed, were hiding in plain sight in various extremist groups, ready to come together under one androgynous uniform when his moment was right: the same cropped hair, the same clothes, same banners and flags, and the same chanted anthems. This gender-neutral Praetorian Guard waited in the wings, primed to commit any atrocity sanctioned by his authority. They had stored up hatred and their hatred would soon be fed. Public disorder, choreographed by his lieutenants to give the impression of social breakdown, would be stamped out by his easily recognisable Guard; his stock as a saviour would soon be on everyone's lips, and his face applauded on every television and cinema screen. The internet would then be both his servant and his showcase, and he would answer calls to give the country the leadership it so desperately needed; he would be ready to seize power in the name of the people. The older man recognised this age-old pattern and he knew that it worked.

A depleted police service, hollowed out by cuts and political correctness, would follow any official line coming from the government website, and control of the organs of state, including the judiciary, the military, and the police, would fall into his hands. Eliminating all resistance, 'The Dark Project' would meld the population into one compliant mass, and disappearances and state sanctioned murder would become the order. To hide his secrets and lies the younger man had surrounded his soul with a hedge of obfuscation, but the older man had brushed this aside like a thicket of smoke and quickly established the true intentions: he had been doing this for long enough not to be fooled by someone whom he regarded as a boy - but a boy who represented a significant threat to the future - and who's attempt at secretiveness had provided the final proof. It was clear to the older man that the younger man had to go: power for its own sake makes a very poor master, and the younger man's ambitions would ultimately lead to a new apocalypse and countless innocent deaths.

The log had almost burned itself to disintegration and was dropping fine white ash into the hearth - breathing its last - when the younger man spoke. He admitted to confusion over the older man's earlier claim that the older man had been blind since birth, and wondered how he could realistically see inside other people? The older suggested that only the blind see presciently, because they are not distracted by the mundanity of vision. Both men swirled their port, lost in different thoughts, then sipped again. The younger enjoyed wine. The older savoured the sun's power combining with the elemental earth, heard solar flares, smelled centuries of custom and tradition, and tasted history as eons flew by. Women's laughter tantalised as the pickers held their end of season party, standing amongst the unburdened vines and feeling stony soil through thin Summer shoes. He sensed fecundity as an ephemeral wind rattled skeletal leaves: in the passing of an unseen hand next year's grapes were formed.

They both swallowed and the deadly poison worked its way into the younger man's system. His end would come very soon and be instantaneous; this because the older man's blindness would disadvantage him and render him vulnerable should the younger man suspect. But the older man was far too practised - too experienced and accomplished - and the younger man had disarmed himself with conceit. His downfall was in agreeing to this very private meeting at which he would be eliminated.

The older man had not dwelled upon the special ones, the ones who minded the fires and fed good people the right fuel, or who burned out the bad ones. He was one of these minders and had chosen his victim through deep research and thought. Smiling inwardly he allowed himself congratulations at ridding the world of another would-be monster, and his thoughts turned to corrupt politicians and a certain cabinet minister. The poison rushed to its work and attacked vigorously, and the wind sighed as the end game played out. Spluttering faint and weak, the log dropped and expired.

An Inner Need

by *Alan Grant*

Michael's expression was the gloomiest she'd ever seen. In the ten years that Claire had been a relationship counsellor, it was not unusual to have to respond to tearful individuals who found the experience quite difficult, even challenging. Responses could range from anger and recriminations through to emotional outbursts, occasional threats, simple resignation and sometimes, as with Michael, a deep at times, almost impenetrable sadness.

Whilst such behaviour, might indicate a depressive illness and require support from a GP, Claire was used to working through the recognised phases of a relationship breakdown. What she found so difficult with Michael, was that his sadness was so deeply entrenched. She also knew instinctively, that she was capable of falling in love, with the vulnerable man in the opposite chair, and felt a deep affinity. There was something in his mannerisms and vulnerability that aroused deep protective feelings within her. He was so reminiscent of Paul, even dressing in the same casual style she'd loved.

In her intensive training, the dangers of Counsellor and Client relationships were key issues. However, as a single parent with teenage children, after Paul's death 5 years ago, and despite long periods of loneliness and grief, Claire had never felt the need for another partner. She'd carried out many such interviews and managed to retain an objective professional approach to her work, whilst meeting a variety of attractive men, all seeking to rebuild their lives; until Michael that is.

His wife Jennifer, made the first appointment. Initially, and over several weeks, Claire provided support and counselling just to her. Michael was simply a figure in the background. However through Jennifer, she gradually came to understand their lifestyle, behaviour and needs. Later she saw them together, cautiously over several weeks, before having individual sessions and joint sessions with them both.

Reflecting on her experience as a Counsellor, Claire felt this family situation had different, perhaps more challenging dimensions than she was used to; so was determined to explore this at a later date. However, what became clear quite quickly, was that the image of Michael, as presented by Jennifer, was quite different from her own perception.

They were in their mid-40's married for 15 years, and from similar professional and social backgrounds. Whilst Jennifer was slightly more reticent, both said the lack of children in the marriage was not a problem; otherwise, it was a familiar situation. After weekly sessions for nearly 2 months, Claire felt she was developing a reasonable understanding of their marital history and subsequent difficulties.

At their latest session, she was therefore, taken aback when Jennifer said otherwise. It happened during a difficult joint session which became angry and recriminatory.

'You're taking sides. Aren't you?' said Jennifer. 'What you've assumed is quite wrong'

'What do you mean?' Claire replied hesitantly.

'When I first met you, we talked about what help you could provide us, and how we could use that help, or not. Do you remember?'

'Of course I do Jennifer. I also said for both it might be a difficult and potentially demanding journey and that at times you might feel like this.'

'Well Claire, I need to tell you that I'm becoming quite anxious in your presence. It *feels* as if you're seeking to go beyond our initial agreement.'

'What do you think that agreement was?'

Jennifer did not respond although her face became quite flushed. There was a distinct silence in the room. After a few moments, Claire turned to Michael. He was looking down at the floor, self consciously, barely acknowledging that Jennifer had spoken at all, let alone responding to her comments. Claire spoke.

'Michael, you haven't said much. We've been looking at your relationship difficulties and it would be helpful to know, what you think about the concerns, that Jennifer has just expressed. What's your view?'

He hesitated, as she knew he would. Beads of perspiration were forming on his forehead. He brushed his thick brown hair to one side, absorbing the moisture in the same motion, then rubbed his soft, well manicured hands on his dark green cord trousers, and grasped his knees. Michael took a deep breath, and pushed his body gently back into the armchair.

'Well I guess what Jennifer is concerned about, is that the more we talk about the past the less chance we have for a future.' He turned towards her. 'Jennifer, it's become clear to me that we've drifted significantly apart, and whilst neither of us wanted it, that's what's actually happened. As for Claire; I don't understand?' Jennifer interrupted.

'Claire, what Michael has just said, isn't what I'm talking about. I'm very concerned that you, our Counsellor, are beginning to use our relationship problems to meet your own needs.'

'What are you talking about Jennifer?' Claire could feel anger rising within her and knew she was responding inappropriately, and despite the years of training, her professional values were fast disappearing. Her response angered Jennifer even more.

'Claire. I'm not blind, nor am I stupid. I know what sensitive issues you and I have discussed with a clear understanding, that the content was confidential between us. How do you think I felt, when I realised that Michael had somehow become aware of my deepest, most private thoughts and feelings about him? In reality, you know a hell of a lot about us, whilst we know absolutely nothing about you.'

Claire felt a blush spreading across her face and neck, and sensing her anxiety levels rising, tried increasing her breathing in response. Pausing, she turned towards Michael, and tried to engage his eyes. He looked away, towards the window, as Claire spoke.

'Jennifer I'll respond to what you've just said in a moment, but first Michael, what have you said that has made Jennifer so angry with me?'

Michael remained silent for a few moments, then shrugged his shoulders, and finally looked up at her. She saw once again the

61

sadness in his eyes, with a tear forming and glistening on the surface and so wanted to reach out and absorb his distress. Michael grasped the arms of his chair; there was a noticeable tremor in his voice.

'Claire, I'm really sorry. Jennifer has totally misread the situation, and what she heard from me, was nothing to do with you. I promise.' Jennifer responded angrily.

'Don't you apologise to her on my behalf Michael. I know what you said and when you said it.' Jennifer looked at Claire triumphantly, seeking a response. 'Including, what happened later, when you were still in our marital bed.'

Claire began to feel anxious again. She knew she was losing it, and that the recriminations between Jennifer and Michael had turned the clock back months. However, it was all also focused on her and she was watching a relationship breakdown accelerate, into complete disarray in front of her eyes, knowing that at least one of them, believed it was her responsibility. Her mind was racing. What could she do to retrieve the situation? What exactly had Jennifer seen or been told?

'Jennifer, Michael, it might be helpful if we have a short break for a few minutes. Let's have cup of coffee, and hopefully things will calm down. Jennifer I promise I will respond to what you've just said, but I feel that if we continue with this anger, and in this way, all the hard work that you've put in over months, will be lost.' She paused. 'Are you both OK on that?'   Jennifer's response was immediate.

'No I'm not! You're avoiding the issue Claire, and you know it. Apart from what Michael has told me, I've seen you with my own eyes. The way you look at him. Sympathising whilst hardly listening to me. Believing everything he says. Who knows what you've been up to, when you've been on your own with him. Well, there are some things you don't know about him that might change your mind.'

'Jennifer stop this now, please' said Michael leaning forward anxiously in his chair. Claire could see a vein pulsing in his forehead, and he was looking distinctly anxious.

'Come on let's go home' he said brusquely. 'We'll talk about

it there.' He began to rise from his chair. Jennifer responded.
'No Michael. No more secrets.'
'What do you mean? Secrets?' asked Claire
'Jennifer. No. Please' said Michael.

She stood up, picked up her coat and handbag and turned towards the door. Then looking directly at Claire.

'You know why we can't have any children Claire. However, ask him about the ones he's got on his PC, in his special place, and then you'll really know the reason why our marriage is breaking down.'

The door slammed behind her. Claire looked into Michael's dark brown eyes for the last time, and finally understood the sadness. The tears that fell were her own.

The Visit

*by **Alan Grant***

As the door slowly swung back on its hinges, a small pile of junk mail offered some resistance, before surrendering and spreading across the floor. There was an immediate impression of gloom and the smell of mould. The darkness in the hallway, emphasised the neglect, which permeated the whole building. Peeling embossed wallpaper, engorged on the dampness of the building, superimposed with decades of smells, from cooking, coal fires, cigarettes, animals and human presence, clung perilously to the surface of the adjacent walls; ready to be peeled and display a heritage of neglect.

A pair of discarded red Wellington boots, suitable for a child or perhaps Paddington Bear lay on the linoleum covered floor near the front door, just below a neglected, weathered hall stand. The stand itself was empty, apart from a dog's lead which moved gently in the fresh breeze, which had begun to encroach into the house through the open door.

On a nearby hook, attached to a wooden, yellowed board, was a multi-coloured full length plastic raincoat with hood. Despite its dated appearance, it offered a distinct and positive presence in the entrance to the house. Moving quietly down the hall, I looked briefly into the kitchen.

A small pile of washed dishes, pots and cutlery lay on a plastic rack. The cupboard surfaces were surprisingly clean and free of crumbs, kitchen debris or inevitable opened boxes of dog biscuit, awaiting a usually ravenous Buster. Even the tiled floor looked relatively clean, although I could see remnants of his last assault on the food bowl, tucked in beneath the oven door, clearly out of his reach.

The small sitting room was quiet and comfortable. A clock ticked on the mantle piece. Old fashioned floral curtains, clearly in need of a wash, covered a fly blown window and greyish net curtains strung on a white plastic wire. The dark smudges of damp on the bottom of the nets, were already beginning to creep upwards. An early autumnal day, was allowing weak sunlight to invade the glass, before entering and embracing the room and its contents.

Despite the cold, I didn't shiver, and moved towards the back door. This led onto an enclosed courtyard. Several seagulls, feasting on the contents of the black bags which lay unattended, sensing my presence immediately took flight. Having examined the back gate of the property, I saw the catch was still in the locked position.

Moving back into the property, and returning towards the front door, I realised that even in the space of a few moments since my arrival, someone had called at the property and pushed mail through the letterbox. The envelope was addressed to me, and came from the Her Majesty's Revenue and Taxes. Predictable, unfailing in their diligence, and guaranteed to have given grief at some stage, to my entire family, friends and extended network. Today it was my turn. Today though, I would ignore them.

It was time to go upstairs. I climbed the steps carefully. Riser number four invariably creaked, irrespective of which side or position, my foot adopted. Today was different: no creak. I was able to quickly progress past riser nine and eleven before reaching the landing and turning right. The bathroom lay immediately ahead. As I approached, I recognised the familiar sound of my constantly dripping sink tap.

It had been a balance, between the minuscule loss of water over a 24 hour period, barely a gallon a week, or the daunting and horrendous cost, of replacing the antiquated plumbing systems within the building. The latter would inevitably require a complete removal of various coppered joints, and external fixtures at massive expense - and for what?

Besides, the sound of a dripping tap was quite reassuring and metronomic. I could stay in bed and time my breathing whilst checking my pulse within the slow, deliberate, drip, drip, drip of the tap. Some people had Grandfather clocks: I had my 1950's Travis

Perkins' white enamelled sink and WC. Turning back I approached the doors leading to the two adjacent bedrooms.

Both appeared closed, however as I got closer, I became aware of a distinct odour. The first bedroom, next to the bathroom, was used by visiting friends or relatives and deliberately sparsely furnished. When no one else was in occupation, it was Buster's Boudoir, and even carried a plaque, acknowledging his status, bought on a day trip to Blackpool. Our coach had disgorged 60 pensioners from Plymouth, alongside a shopping mall, in the midst of torrential rain. The plaque was irresistible.

Today, Buster was clearly absent. His boudoir whilst empty, was clean and ready, to receive guests. Moving towards the main bedroom, the odour became even stronger. This door also appeared closed, yet pushed opened easily in response to my impending presence.

Buster lay in his basket adjacent to the door. He was completely emaciated. His tongue, now dark blue rather than a healthy red, had congealed into a small lump protruding from between his teeth, onto his lower jaw. His eyes were glazed, unfocused, blank, yet intact. I moved into the room just as a flurry of bluebottles, suddenly lifted off the bed, and cascaded into the air, before diving through the open door and plummeting downwards in co-ordinated movements, before escaping the house through the still opened front door. It was reminiscent of the familiar flights of flocks of starlings.

The bed held a dark, swollen torso with a blackened face covered in larvae, with dead bluebottles surrounding it. I stooped closer. Unlike Buster, there were no eyes left in the skull of this cadaver, and yet it was still familiar. On a shrunken wrist, where bones emerged from the withered parchment skin, was a familiar object. The second hands were still turning, although the accompanying bracelet was already showing signs of distress. On an adjacent bedside table, lay two gold rings, one for engagement and the other a wedding ring. I Instinctively wanted to reach out and touch them.

The bedroom door slowly swung to and I saw the obvious desperation of Buster, who over many days, had clearly tried to

66

escape by flinging himself at it. Deep claw marks, rising from the bottom plinth, to halfway up the surface of the door, evidenced his frantic attempts, before he finally retreated into his basket and final sleep.

The stench from the cadaver was now quite overwhelming. I stood up and moved towards the door. How much longer until my death was established? I needed to move onto my new world. Hurry up someone. Find me!

A Personal Passion

by *Alan Grant*

The blue flashing light was the usual announcement of his impending approach. As Head of CID, Dean might be uncertain about what would confront him on arrival, however, the journey to the scene of crime itself, was one of complete exhilaration. His driver Jason, would achieve massive speeds with complete disregard for public limits, or the needs of other road users, whilst reinforcing a clear police privilege when going to work.

The sudden arrival of an emblazoned white car with blue flashing lights sitting unexpectedly behind them, would usually create a feeling of anxiety. Although most drivers were totally innocent, the usual reaction, after the brake lights flashed on, was a sharp rise in personal stress until the police vehicle accelerated past.

There were already a number of police cars at the scene. They were parked haphazardly, their blue flashing lights defining the boundary of the investigation, with yellow fluorescent tape protecting the immediate surroundings. DCI Dean Street stepped carefully out of his car. He'd ceased to be surprised at the public image of incompetent uniformed policemen, on routine traffic duties, being suddenly thrust into a major murder investigation because of their proximity to a reported incident. Nothing could be further from the truth. They were trained police officers, first and foremost, with significant skills.

It might be several hours before a specialist forensic team reached the scene, during which time, a poorly secured boundary at an incident, could allow key evidence to be missed, or obliterated by subsequent arrivals. This time he was quite impressed, as newly appointed Detective Sergeant Sonia Amis, approached. She was in her early 30's, and recently transferred from Scotland.

She'd been part of his team for three months, and had already demonstrated a visible enthusiasm in respect of her duties which impressed him. Her experience of working in Glasgow CID

68

was quite evident. They shook hands and he was reminded of the strength and intensity of her grip.

'Hello Sonia. What've we got?'

'I've been on scene for over an hour boss, and extended the parameter beyond the original boundaries. At about 11 o'clock this morning a lorry driver needed to take a leak.
He couldn't face the prospect of a further 40 miles to the next service station, so decided to pull onto the hard shoulder, put his hazard warning lights on, then continue once he'd been.'

'And?'

'Well as he nipped up the adjacent embankment and entered the trees, he stumbled across the body of a young woman. She was completely naked, and appears to have died from asphyxiation. It was pure coincidence that she was found. This is a very isolated part of the motorway. She could have lain here for years. Scenes of crime have covered the immediate area with their tentage. Photographers are on site, and I've been in touch with the duty Pathologist.'

'Who is it?'

She smiled. 'Professor Stevens. And guess what he said?'

'Something about big footed thick coppers trampling all over the place I guess. But we're lucky, he's the best in the business, so we need to indulge him. OK Sonia, let's have a look shall we?'

Dean moved carefully up the adjacent embankment. Although both the hard standing and inside lane of the motorway were closed, he was sensitive to the constant movement and noise of vehicles behind him. He wondered if the killer was at this very moment driving by, checking out the scene, not realising that a chance call of nature for a lorry driver, had begun a murder enquiry.

Dean was now completely in charge, and responsible for the investigation. A successful outcome would be dependant on his team's skills and experience, together with reliable forensic evidence, and occasionally even a large slice of luck. Standard police procedures covered most eventualities, yet he knew every murder was unique, whether in motive, method, location or victim.

The two masked, white suited and hooded Scenes of Crime officers, looking like workers in a nuclear plant, shuffled busily within the confines of their tented area. They looked up briefly and nodded, as he entered their space and stood discretly watching the activities. This was his second piece of encouragement. Lee Pearce and Mandy Court were the most experienced members of the County Task Force, and together with Professor Stevens would provide him with a formidable team in respect of quality evidence and facts. If any existed, they'd find it.

She lay on her back stark naked, her face partly concealed by long blond hair, which appeared to have been deliberately placed in position. The lower torso was defined by a mound of dark pubic hair which appeared to have been shaven on the edges. Her limbs did not indicate a person who had simply been dumped. They were arranged carefully, the legs drawn up slightly, and to one side, with both ankles touching. Her right hand rested gently on the rib cage just below her breasts. The left hand appeared to be reaching out as far as possible to the side of her body, the palm open and knuckles down. Both hands were bereft of any jewellery or rings. The fingers were bruised. There was no sign of female clothing.

Without the distinct purple mottling of the skin around her throat, she might have been asleep, unaware of the attention she was receiving, and simply enjoying the summer sunshine in the presence of voyeurs. Professor Stevens would provide a judicial, scientific conclusion on death, with importantly, possible time frames. Meanwhile Dean had seen enough strangulated women to recognise the cause.

There was already one irrefutable fact. Once again, his three children might be disappointed that he wouldn't be with them during the impending school holidays. The increasing tension with his wife Helen would also be aggravated. Dean always took additional holiday insurance, and had previously claimed for the first problem. The second was uninsurable. He was hungry, and could still remember the smell of lunch roasting in the oven, and his mumbled apologies, as his wife opened the front door in response to today's emergency.

He began to reach for his mobile phone. There was no possibility of getting back home tonight, and whilst apologising, he wouldn't talk to Helen about disrupting the holiday just yet. That would be difficult enough, if it happened. As he began to dial, he saw Lee Pearce rising purposefully to his feet, and walking towards him, pulling the white mask down below his chin. Dean pressed the pause button on his mobile.

Lee now had a permanent stubble of greying hair. It'd been at least 10 years since they'd first started working together, and thoughts of his own image flashed before him. Did he also look so middle-aged and tired? 'Anything? Lee?'

Lee shrugged his shoulders. As usual, he was non-committal, preferring instead to describe the options and leave it to the 'experts in CID' to decide what to do. This time however, despite the usual shrug and shoulder movement, Dean saw a distinct sense of purpose in Lee's eyes. Something was up, and yet Lee still needed to enjoy the moment.

'Yes and No.' said Lee slowly and deliberately. 'What'd you want first Dean?' his face breaking into a smile.

'Lee. With you, there's always lots of No's.' said Dean impatiently. 'No evidence, no this, no that, no nothing. Gimme a "Yes" you bastard! Please.'

'OK' said Lee. He paused, and drew a deep breath. 'I've seen it before.'

'Seen what?' said Dean, his frustration beginning to rise. He took a deep breath as visions of cancelled holidays and disappointed children again began to enter his thinking.

'The deceased layout. Positioning the legs and arms, moving the blond hair across the eyes. I've seen it before. It must have been in the early 90's. I've been working in Devon for at least 10 years. I was in the Met before I moved down here. We put him away for life with a 15 year minimum. He did at least two women. Both the same. Long blond hair. Kept their rings. Weird. Got life. I remember standing in court and watching him go down. Nasty sod. Don't forget people like that in a hurry.' He paused momentarily. 'Nixon. That was his name!' he said triumphantly. 'He must be about 50+ nowadays. Now let's find the DNA.'

Detective Sergeant Amis needed no further bidding. She ran to the Incident Control Vehicle and activated the onboard computer. Ten minutes later, she walked back dejectedly, and re-entered the

71

tent. Her soft Scottish accent made her response more poignant.

'Sorry boss. Nixon is still in custody. Can't have been him.'

'Where is he now?'

'Leyhill. Been there over 12 months.'

'Sonia. Do you know what Leyhill is, and not only that .....where it is?' said Dean, visibly trying to control his excitement.

'Dunno boss.' she replied, puzzled, watching his expression move from disappointment to exhilaration.

'Get the car' he exclaimed. 'Get the car ready Sonia!'

'Why boss?'

'Leyhill is an Open Prison some 60 miles away with minimal prisoner supervision. That includes previously banged up Murderers and Rapists. Our Mr Nixon is clearly in need of a visit. Especially if he's back in his cell, thinking he's safe.'

Retribution

*by **John L. Horsham***

Nathan Wesley was the youngest of three brothers who arrived in the Far East with their parents in 1940. His father was to become the Production Manager in Singapore Royal Naval Dockyard. Leo Wesley; Nathan's father had landed this plum promotion in recognition of his stellar performance at the open examination for entry into the Royal Corps of Naval Constructors. He had topped the national examination list by achieving an average mark of 98% for the set of five papers! His rise from his humble origins as a young Shipwright through various junior and middle management positions to senior rank, was regarded as, meteoric.

An added bonus for the family was, with the country at war, Leo Wesley would be required to wear Naval Uniform. Whilst young Nathan was barely three years old his abiding lifetime memory was seeing his father for the first time smartly turned out in his sparkling white tropical uniform with three gold bars on his epaulettes. The whole family shared in the status accorded to his position. Their bungalow, by comparison to the dingy flat they had rented in Devonport, was both spacious and exotic! The family was served by an 'Amma', who was essentially a Housekeeper who cooked and cleaned for them all. The social life was one long round of pleasure for Nathan's mother who had been released from her 'hands on' parental duties of caring for three young boys. Cocktail Parties, sea, sunshine and wonderful food. Life was almost too good to be true. ---- And it was!

Sadly, their sojourn in this Shangri La was destined to be short lived. Nathan could hardly help overhearing conversations between the many adults who frequently passed through his house. He had also heard the local children chattering in hushed voices about the advance of the feared Japanese. Rumours were rife! He regularly quizzed his Father about this enemy of their much vaunted British Empire. Leo Wesley always laughed at his young son's fears over the possibility of an attack by the Imperial Army of Japan! He reassured him that there was absolutely no chance that any enemy would ever be able to overcome the powerful defences of the British Forces in Singapore! Leo Wesley was soon to learn that his assurances to his young son were worthless.

In February 1942, the day after Nathan's fourth birthday, his whole world changed. Singapore fell to the invading forces of the Emperor Hirohito! Catastrophic errors of military strategy and judgement had led to the disaster; the defences of the City had been installed to repel a Naval Assault from the sea! Huge artillery guns and Pill Boxes all pointed seaward and could not be rotated to face the rear! Whilst Singapore was impregnable from the sea, the resourceful Japanese had completely outflanked the British defences by mounting a lightning strike from the inland jungle. Their assault had been achieved by transporting themselves hundreds of miles at incredible speed on bicycles! Nathan could not understand why the British General had surrendered after a mere token defence! The memory of seeing columns of British, Australian and Indian soldiers being Force Marched away; to he knew not where, became etched upon his young psyche. An even more indelible memory was the sight of his father being assaulted with the butt of a rifle by a diminutive Japanese soldier! Then; without even the benefit of a farewell hug, his father was gone! Taken; as he was later to learn, to work on the construction of a Bridge. In order to lighten the blow of losing his father, his mother lied and said that he would return at the end of the war. It transpired that it would be the last time Nathan was ever to see him, Leo Wesley reportedly died from the effects of; disease, forced labour and starvation.

Nathan, together with his brothers and mother were taken to a camp 40 miles deep into the impenetrable jungle where they were to suffer cruelty, hunger and degradation. They languished for the next three and half years in abject despair!

Memories of those early years had remained with Nathan throughout his life. However, by the age of fifty- the traumas relived in his nightmares had subsided and as he settled down into his comfortable Business Class seat on a flight from Heathrow to Tokyo accompanied by his younger brother Oliver, he fell into a fitful sleep. The disturbing memories of those unforgettable years of imprisonment, as they regularly did, once again permeated into his dreams. He had resolved to himself as a small boy that he would one day seek retribution from his cruel captors. He would exact revenge on one man in particular and would make him bow before him, as he and his brothers had been forced to do hundreds of times during their incarceration. Through the influence of his younger brother, Nathan finally discovered that Lieutenant Kenzo Yokomura, the Camp Interpreter and second in command, was indeed, still alive!

Through his many contacts within Japanese industry, Oliver had managed to contact the 71 year old Yokomura who was living on the island of Honshu. He had after the war, spent 10 years in a Military Prison. Thereafter, he had returned to Post War Japan and carved out a career in the rapidly expanding motor car industry. Nathan was amazed to learn that according to Oliver, Yokomura had without any persuasion, agreed to see them! Whilst the lifelong flame of revenge in his troubled mind, had over the years eased to mere glowing embers of resentment, Nathan was resolute in his determination to exact overdue retribution. In his teens he had vowed that whatever the consequences, he would, if ever the opportunity arose, kill the man who during those dark times had earned himself the sobriquet of; 'the Iceman'. He had earned this odd nickname due to his calm and dispassionate persona. He had never displayed any signs of anger when administering or ordering physical punishment. He was inscrutable! Oliver remembered nothing of the years his family had spent in captivity. He had in fact been born in the camp in 1945, just before the Japanese surrender in August of that year! However, due to the stories related to him by his brothers after the war, he was as determined as Nathan to exact retribution for the mal treatment his family had suffered at the hands of the man they loathed with a passion.

It was disconcerting for Nathan to come to terms with the fact that the reason for the survival of his family was due in part to the covertly favourable treatment they had received by way of extra food and medication, courtesy of their *bête noire*; Kenzo Yokomura! Whether it was to her credit, or to her shame, was ever thereafter a matter for conjecture, but Edith Wesley had resolved that whatever the price she might be called upon to pay, she would see her boys survive their ordeal which was to claim the lives of many other children.

Edith Wesley was an attractive woman who was possessed of a strong religious faith but had never the less succumbed to the pressure of becoming Yokomura's concubine! Consequently, she was reviled by other prisoners for her seemingly willing fraternisation with the enemy. And when she fell pregnant during the final months of the war she became *persona non grata*. Whilst Nathan and his brothers were also regarded as being somehow complicit in their mother's conduct, their loyalty to her never wavered. They stoically shared the brunt of disapproval meted out to them by fellow prisoners.

Lieutenant Yokomura only ever had a fleeting opportunity to see his baby son shortly after Edith had given birth. And Nathan could clearly remember his uncharacteristic emotion, as with tears in his eyes he was whisked away to Changi Prison on the day following Oliver's birth! After a perfunctory trial with its inevitable verdict, he remained incarcerated there for 10years until 1955. His only possession during his long ordeal was a copy of the King James Bible!

The widow; Edith Wesley, to her eternal credit declined the opportunity to abandon baby Oliver. She insisted that he, like her, was an innocent casualty of War and that she intended to raise him with his three elder half brothers! Thus; the mixed race child, *Oliver James Wesley* together with his family, sailed for England. They eventually arrived back in the City of Plymouth just in time for Christmas 1945. The family was extremely fortunate to find anywhere to live as the City had been devastated by heavy bombing during the wartime Blitz. Edith had by chance encountered a sympathetic Council Employee in the housing department who mentioned to her that she knew of a sickly and aged farmer who needed one - to - one care. Thus it was that Edith, who had been a nurse prior to her marriage to Leo Wesley, was taken on as the old man's carer. Both she and her boys looked after old Donald Hutchins as if he were family. He often said that his twilight years with the Wesley family were the happiest of his life. The family thrived on the little farm in the oddly named village of Eggbuckland until their elderly charge died in 1955. Whilst Edith Wesley inherited the farm, it was subject to a Compulsory Purchase Order shortly thereafter. The land had been requisitioned by the Local Authority to build a new school and housing to cater for the explosion in the numbers of children in the era of the post war 'Baby Boomer' generation.

Whilst life in the immediate decade after the war was a time of privation and rationing in Britain, the Wesley boys thought by comparison to the hardships they had endured as prisoners of the Emperor, it was a land of milk and honey! When their classmates at school learned of their story, they became minor celebrities. Young Oliver had a striking appearance, inheriting as is often the case, the best features of both his biological parents. However, with his mother's fair hair and his father's contrasting Asiatic features he looked quite different from his peers and from the moment he started school, he was bullied. He was reviled as some kind of freak and was accorded the nickname; Tojo, the renowned Japanese General! However, one of his brothers was always on hand to act as his protector and Nathan in particular never ducked a fight in his little brother's defence. The bond between them became extremely strong. They adopted the motto of the Three Musketeers; *All for one and one for all*! Oliver styled himself as D'Artagnan; the Fourth Musketeer! He eventually blossomed into a celebrity in his own right as he not only excelled at every kind of Sport, he was also a brilliant student with a flair for languages. He was even selected at Scrum Half to represent the England School Boys Rugby Team! One after the other the Wesley boys passed the scholarship examination and attended the City's Premier Grammar School. Thereafter, they all then secured university places. Alexander, the eldest opted for a career in the Church and subsequently became a Bishop. He had long found it within himself to forgive the sins of the past. Christopher was sadly reported missing in action at the age of twenty one fighting in Korea during his National Service.

As the stewardess came down the aisle Oliver awakened his sleeping brother with a nudge; *Trolly Dolly Bro*; *grub up*. Nathan stretched his arms behind his head and smiled. He had often mused to himself how it could possibly be that such a loving and devoted sibling was the result of an unholy union between his mother and Kenzo Yokomura. He had over the years often looked for signs of Yokomura's evil seed within his charismatic younger brother, but there was never a trace, he was; generous to a fault, gregarious, funny, loyal, intelligent and infinitely resourceful. Oliver had in fact far outshone his brothers in terms of success in life, he had won a scholarship to Oxford and obtained a rare 'Double First', he had even acted as *Cox* to the victorious Oxford Boat Race Crew! Whilst he had Degrees in both Languages and Business Administration it was never the less reckoned as exceptionally good fortune at his young age to have gained such a prized appointment with the Japanese arm of the *Shell Oil Company*. At his interview for the position he had sensed a certain warmth and empathy from the selection panel and chuckled to his pals afterwards that he had, 'charmed the pants off them'! It was almost as if the exercise had been a mere formality! It was suggested to him by his brothers that he had probably found favour due to his Japanese heritage! Oliver responded by indignantly stating that if that was indeed the case, it was a long overdue payback for all the grief that it had caused him as a boy. He quickly demonstrated his mercurial talents by rapidly climbing the managerial ladder on sheer merit and ingenuity! At the age of 42 he became Managing Director in the Company's Far East operations!

By comparison, Nathan who had always been regarded as something of a plodder, opted for a safer passage in life and became a teacher of Engineering Design. He had retired early due to stress and psychological problems which his Doctors opined were not unrelated to the traumas experienced in his early years. Oliver; or O.J. as he had come to be universally known, insisted that he could land him a plum position within *Shell Oil* and he had arranged this particular trip to Japan for this express purpose. Whilst this bothered Nathan slightly, he couldn't resist his young brother's enthusiasm to show him a world he had never seen. Oliver of course had long since cracked the secret of his controversial origins and consequently bore an unwarranted burden of guilt; he harboured a burning resentment against his biological father. He also felt ashamed of his nagging sense of curiosity about the man who had so abused his beloved mother. He felt that any interest he might show would be seen as a disloyalty by the family that he loved. He further bore a burden of guilt at certain perplexing knowledge gained whilst acting as Executor of his mother's Will. Edith Wesley had died at the relatively young age of 66 and Oliver had yet to muster the courage to share this information with his brothers. Secrecy weighed heavily on his conscience.

Nathan was gripped by doubts as to just what he and Oliver might do when they eventually met the demon who had cast such a shadow over their lives! He was also troubled by several irreconcilable contradictions in his past memories. He had through the years grudgingly come to accept that had it not been for his mother's association with Yokomura, he would not have survived. He had contracted malaria in 1943 and would certainly have perished but for the Quinine which had been secretly smuggled to her! A further memory which he found difficult to rationalise was that Yokomura had undoubtedly taken many risks on behalf of the Wesley family during their incarceration! Despite this Nathan could not forgive the fact that his vulnerable widowed mother had undoubtedly been seduced by a lustful man who exercised absolute power over her; it was for this unmitigated abuse that he reasoned he was honour bound to exact retribution!

Oliver for his part, was also in a state of confusion; his love for his family was unconditional and any enemy of theirs, was an enemy of his. *All for and one for all,* he reminded himself was the fraternal code by which they were bound! He felt a debt of familial duty towards them all and he resolved to himself, that regardless of the consequences, he would play his part in any act of retribution that Nathan was contemplating. However, upon the death of their mother in 1980 the contents of her private treasure chest had thrown Oliver's mind into turmoil. The box which was full of secret letters and personal effects had shaken him to his very core!

On top of the pile of papers he had discovered a sepia photograph of an Officer of the Japanese Imperial Army! It could only be that of his biological father; Kenzo Yokomura! It stunned him. He slammed the wooden box shut and sat deep in thought for a few minutes. Moreover, it was also a face which was vaguely familiar to him. Just what it was doing nestling in the box of treasured effects of his beloved mother was beyond his understanding! Oliver reasoned that he had a duty to read the sheaf of letters in order to make sense of the presence of the photograph. Thereafter he wrestled with the problem of how he would tell his brothers what he had discovered.

After landing in Tokyo the two brothers were driven by chauffeured limousine to a five star hotel. Nathan was astounded at the largesse of Oliver's company expense account. They dined together in the evening and he was once again taken aback by his resourceful little brother who chatted to the Concierge and Reception staff at the hotel in what appeared to be fluent Japanese! Oliver smiled broadly at the look of astonishment on his brother's face. *Sorry Bro. I kept that one quiet, I thought I'd better learn the lingo as it seems I'll be here working for quite a few years.* Nathan responded with his voice full of admiration; *Christ, O.J. is there anything you can't do? ---- French, Greek, German, Spanish and now Japanese, that's 5 bloody languages!* Oliver flashed his rakish smile and said; *don't forget English Bro. I'm pretty good at that too!* Nathan raised his eyebrows and replied in a faintly exasperated tone; *Okay you little Smart Ass, I give in, you win -- again!*

After a meal fit for a king and copious amounts of fine wine Oliver suggested to his brother that they adjourn to his suite for coffee and brandy. They both sank into their respective plush armchairs close to an ornate bamboo table with a glass top. Nathan's eyes quickly settled on the plain teak box which Oliver had placed where it could be clearly seen. Nathan exclaimed;-- *Mother's Box! What the hell is it doing here in Japan?* Oliver quietly said; *not too sure Bro. but I think we should perhaps investigate further don't you?* Nathan looked intently into his young brother's eyes, he sensed that his carefully measured words were an indication that there was a plot afoot, but never the less nodded his silent assent.

Oliver turned the key to the box and invited his brother to open it! As Nathan slowly raised the lid his eyes immediately fell upon the sepia photograph of Kenzo Yokomura. He froze! *What in God's name is that doing in mother's box of treasures?* Oliver remained silent until he whispered; *what indeed my dear Bro? What indeed? Shall we investigate by reading the letters, which as you see, all bear a Japanese post mark?*

Oliver took the initiative and for the ensuing hour slowly re-read the contents to his stunned brother. The letters were all dated and written in a beautiful Copper-plate Script, they spanned the 35 years between 1945 and 1980. They were the most tender love letters that perhaps only a poet could have crafted. Each letter carried a footnote referring to a not inconsiderable cash remittance made by Yokomura in favour of Edith Wesley! Oliver had managed to hold his composure throughout, but Nathan bit his lip, turned his head and shed silent tears aplenty.

They sat in silence for a good 30minutes, each alone with his thoughts, pondering the implications of the secret love letters. Surprisingly; it was Nathan who eventually rose from his chair and said; *well that's a relief, we won't have to kill the little bastard now!* Oliver also confessed his relief at having to forego the task of murdering his own father! *Not that we will ever see them Bro.* whispered Oliver, *but you do realise that the letters from mother would have been equally as intimate as those we have just read? What intrigues me most is the reference to the Bible she apparently gave him!* Nathan nodded sagely and expressed his tremendous relief at being finally able to admit to always having suppressed doubts over the assumed evil nature of Lieutenant Yokomura who he recalled had often restrained and reprimanded his sadistic Corporals from beating prisoners for little, or no reason. The brothers acknowledged to one another that the conduct of Japanese soldiers had been inculcated into them by the uncompromising *Martial Code of; Bushido*! They had all sworn an oath to their Emperor to conduct themselves in the way that they did! Many were undoubtedly cruel by nature, but others like Kenzo Yokomura secretly maintained their innate humanity and as far as they dared, paid mere lip service to the Brutal Edicts of their Warrior Creed!

The four Wesley brothers had always marvelled at just how their mother, surviving on a Naval Pension had managed to support and send her 4 boys to University! They had never wanted for anything! The answer to the conundrum was of course to be found in the cash sent from Japan! Nathan's mind was in turmoil as it became clear that Yokomura had in fact, been their long serving and dutiful Benefactor!

Nathan Wesley slept well that night, he had shed the burden of responsibility for exacting revenge on a man he had loathed all his life. In his dreams he finally accepted what his subconscious had always pressured him to do. He remembered instances when his and Yokomura's eyes had met during his incarceration. Whilst no words were spoken, rather than scorn and hostility, he had sensed sympathy and even warmth! He also remembered that when Red Cross Christmas parcels had been stolen by Japanese Soldiers, it was Yokomura who had recovered them! He further reminded himself of the transformation which had taken place under Yokomura's stewardship of the camp when the Commandant had been transferred to active duty in the final months of the war. He awoke in the morning refreshed and unburdened by the legacy of his tortured past!

At breakfast Oliver could not help but notice the change in his brother's demeanour. Gone were the harassed look and the frown lines. They smiled broadly at one another. They each instinctively sensed that there had been an enlightenment awakened within them. They had both

82

experienced the same Damascene Conversion! The certain knowledge that they no longer bore the burden of having to avenge their mother was a sweet release!

Oliver gave Nathan a VIP tour of his company's installations and indicated that there was a well paid place for him. Nathan smiled at his, 'wheeler dealer brother' and politely declined. *'What do I know about the Oil Industry O.J.? I would be no more than a passenger! Thanks -- but no thanks. Now if you had had the nous to have gone into the Car industry instead of Oil, it would be different, it's something I should have done for myself years ago instead of becoming a teacher!* Oliver stifled a barely audible snigger and a furtive smile which intrigued Nathan; he knew for sure from past experience that his brother was up to something!

It was then that the Machiavellian and ever resourceful O.J. casually said; *'well Bro. I may just be able to help with that particular pipe dream!* Nathan fixed his younger brother with a quizzical look! *I recently met a real 'big shot' who is the Chairman of Nissan Motors and I happened to mention that I was bringing my brother over to Japan in the hope of finding him a suitable position and he said he would very much like to meet you.* Nathan frowned at his brother and said; *and why the hell O.J. would he want to see me?* Oliver responded by saying ; *Well; perhaps I did 'Big you up a bit Bro, but I just happened to mention that you had taught Engineering Design at University for 25years and had invented several revolutionary engine modifications for which you had never been credited and how as a boy of 17, you had built your own Racing Car from scratch. He was impressed.*

Nathan protested that such a mundane C.V. hardly fitted him for consideration by the 'Head Honcho' of Nissan Motors. *Really O.J. I'm nothing special as an Engineer, I'm just a clapped out teacher who's good at tinkering with engines!* Well my dear brother, smirked Oliver, *that's not quite how Mr. Nissan sees things, he has developed a very special interest in you and he is here in the building for the express purpose of meeting you.* Oliver pressed the button on his desk which signalled that the distinguished visitor should be ushered in!

As the door to his office opened Nathan turned to face the visitor. They needed no introduction! There, standing before him stood --- Kenzo Yokomura, Chairman of Nissan Motors who slowly and purposefully bowed to Nathan! As he slowly arose from his act of humble supplication their eyes met for the first time since the war. Oliver with his usual immaculate timing and sense of occasion broke the silence and said;-- *Gentlemen; East meets West once again, I think this calls for a group hug!* The three men embraced for a full minute, with tears of mutual joy and relief freely flowing.

Nathan stayed in Japan for two weeks, both he and Oliver were the personal guests of Nissan Motors and during that time many ghosts were excised from their minds. Kenzo Yokomura sought forgiveness for the sins of his country's past and explained that in the event they had come to inflict retribution, they were in any case, too late. He ruefully added that he had been severely punished for the past 50 years by the burden of his own conscience. Moreover, it was a tortured conscience he had lived with during his 10 long years in Changi Prison with only the Bible given to him by their mother as his comforter! He quietly confessed to having become a Christian!

He explained that he had no children as he had never married. The only one true love of his life had been a certain Edith Wesley and sadly fate had conspired to keep them apart. He further stated that it had been the realisation of his dearest dream when his son Oliver, after half a lifetime had unexpectedly appeared before him whilst he was serving on an Executive Recruitment Panel for Nippon United Industries! Nathan looked at his brother and whispered;-- *O.J. I know that you and me were never too big on religion, but you—you--- were surely Heaven Sent! I seem to remember the good book saying; something like---- Blessed are* ****** Kenzo Yokomura raised his hand so as to pause Nathan in mid sentence; ---then turning to face his son Oliver, completed the Beatitude ;- ***Blessed are the peacemakers for they shall be called the children of God!***

84

RIGHT TO ROAM

*by **Moyra MacKyan***

In general Sir Henry liked young people; he enjoyed their exuberance and bright ideas and admired the fact that they were not afraid to fight for what they believed in. He envied their crusading spirit and their certainty – it saddened him to think that age and experience would rob most of them of these qualities. He especially liked the three youngsters that he had known from childhood; they had always been a threesome and you knew, if you spotted one of them, that the others would not be far behind. He had never come across that kind of friendship between boys and girls when he was growing up; to his generation women were separate, different, a bit scary. Men made friends with other men: drinking together, tinkering with engines and mending things, spending a lot of time outdoors or in the sanctuary of their sheds, brewing lethal concoctions.

Robbie and Sam were nice boys, good sorts that you could trust. Their families had lived here for generations. He enjoyed the camaraderie that developed when they helped him with all the jobs that needed doing around the estate, like rounding up cattle, mending fences or fixing the tractor; having them around made him feel less old. He would allow them into his sanctuary to try the latest rhubarb wine, and they were always polite about it, raising their glasses to the light and admiring the clarity of the liquid, the rich colour and flavour. Sometimes he knew they were being kind about the wine because he, himself, could tell it was not a vintage year, but he was grateful for their kindness and it made their friendship stronger.

He remembered how last year, when Jane was on study leave, she had spent a lot of time bottle feeding the orphaned lambs. She had a lovely way with the animals and took a great interest in farming, about which she had strong views. He enjoyed their lively discussions, which gave him food for thought and prevented him

85

from getting stuck in his ways; it was thanks to her that he had planted two wildflower meadows, something he had stubbornly resisted doing for years. He smiled as he recalled the way he teased her when she got serious about conservation; he would point to one of the hedgerows and threaten to cut it down.

"That hedge has got to go," he would say, shaking his gnarled stick at it. "It takes up far too much of my time keeping it under control." She would turn on him indignantly.

"You can't do that, Uncle Henry, think about all the wildlife, all the hedgehogs, the birds, the dormice, all the little creatures that would have nowhere to go without that hedge. They really, really need that hedge."

"Oh, all right," he would reply, pretending to frown in a curmudgeonly way. "I won't cut it – for now at any rate." He would wink at her and she would reward him with a radiant smile and a hug.

Jane, Sam and Robbie sat in the Plume of Feathers. It was a crowded Saturday night and they were enjoying the atmosphere but their main agenda was to discuss their latest venture; they were searching for a suitable stretch of open water to indulge their new craze. Sam sat bolt upright as a brilliant idea struck him. "I know," he said. "Why don't we use Sir Henry's river?"

Jane frowned. "I don't think we could do that without asking him first. He might get upset, and I wouldn't want to upset him – and nor would you."

"But, Jane, why should he get upset? It's not as if we're planning something bad, or illegal; it's just a dip in the water," Sam countered.

"And," Robbie added, "It's not as if he's never let us swim in it before. We've been in and around that river almost the whole of our lives."

"Well, I don't know. I still think we should ask."

"Oh, come on. If we ask then he's going to want to know why we're suddenly asking, and then he might get suspicious, when the whole point of what we're doing is that it should be a secret."

"I suppose you're right."

"Good, that's that, then. It's decided. Sir Henry's river it is."

They were not to know that others, less considerate than themselves, had already come up with the same idea and had been visiting the river regularly, with their loud, boorish behaviour and complete disregard for the landowner and his livestock, which was driving Sir Henry mad.

Funny how you could not tell the difference between shrieks of fun and screams of fear, Sir Henry observed to no one in particular. He looked up without focussing – he was listening for any sounds; hearing none, he snapped open his newspaper and relaxed.

It was the fourth time this week he had been woken early by loud noises coming from the river that flowed through his estate. He was losing patience with whoever it was; they had no business being on his land anyway – the right to roam had gone too far and something needed to be done. He was tired of governments trying to increase their popularity by letting all and sundry wander about wherever they wanted to; people needed boundaries because, without them, bad things happened and no one took responsibility. Why, just last week he had lost three pregnant ewes to a pack of dogs in a shocking attack that had made him furious. He had seen the owner jogging away, the dogs running all over the place as they followed him, and he had tried to take a photo on his mobile phone but it had not worked, so he tried to run after them but they easily outran him and disappeared. The episode was lodged in his brain and it rankled; something needed to be done about strangers invading his land.

"Robbie, I'm sc ---- ." Jane's voice had been cut off by something powerful and unseen, dragging her down to the river bed. The only evidence of what had occurred was a large circle of bubbles spreading out on the surface of the water.

"Jane, Jane, where are you?" Sam and Robbie were puzzled. They had heard her cries and the loud commotion in the river but everything had suddenly gone eerily quiet; there were no clues as to what might have happened. They decided not to call out any more – their eyes were wide open, their hearts pounding as they scoured the banks for signs of what it might be, or where it was hiding. Sam cleared his throat and whispered, "Do you think it's one of those big cats people talk about?"

"Maybe it's more than one." Robbie replied, the thought of which filled them with dread.

They were trying not to make noise but fear was crowding their minds and drying their mouths and they could not help coughing and clearing their throats. Sobered by the idea that there could be more than one dangerous predator close by, they were glad when they stumbled upon a pile of dead wood and picked out two stout branches which they used to cautiously move the foliage; finding nothing made them bolder and they started to shout and wave the branches about, hoping the thing would run away, but all they found was silence.

Without warning, Sam heard Robbie exclaim and, turning his head, he was just in time to see him being dragged into the river, calling "Help – help me – Sam!" and then silence. Where he had been pulled in, Sam could see a large circle of bubbles racing up to the surface and popping, chased by thousands more bubbles until the surface of the water seethed and boiled, as if something was thrashing about at the bottom of the river bed, but the surface was dark and cloaked in vegetation and Sam could see nothing. After a few moments the river became calm and still again, as if nothing had happened.

"That's no big cat," Sam told himself. "Time to get out of here," but, as he turned to make his way back, something reared up in front of him and, when he registered what it was, his eyes stared with disbelief – a crocodile? He froze and the crocodile lunged. It reared up again and snapped its jaws round his waist, dragging him into the river, where the others joined in the feast till there was nothing left.

Sir Henry was feeling very pleased. During the last two weeks he had not found a single trespasser on his land. The reptiles had done their job and would soon be in their crates and on their way back to Africa. He looked out of the window and sighed with pleasure; the sky was a rich blue and the sun was shining. It was promising to be a wonderful summer.

EYE CANDY

*by **Moyra MacKyan***

Zelda Crane was very proud of her baby. Everybody complimented her on his beauty, his blonde hair and his lovely blue eyes. Complete strangers would stare at him as she wheeled him round the shops. What's his name? They would ask, cooing at him as he smiled and gurgled at them. Marlon, she told them. She had fallen in love with Marlon Brando after seeing "On the Waterfront" at the cinema; his sultry good looks and mesmerising gaze had stayed with her and so choosing a name for her son had been easy. The only difficulty lay in persuading her husband who thought that Marlon sounded effeminate and would have preferred Robert or William but she persevered and, eventually, he gave in.

Marlon spent most of his school life getting into fights while trying to defend his name; not only did he get called a Nancy boy but he also aroused jealousy among the other boys because he could attract any girl he chose without making any effort; all he had to do was give her a look, raise his eyebrows, and she would come running. He was not academic and had no practical ability for things like woodwork, so he ended up drifting through the education system. He was heading nowhere and the future looked bleak.

"Hello, do you mind if I sit here?" He looked up. A very attractive young woman stood opposite him, gesturing at the empty chair. She did not sound like anyone from round here, she sounded posh. He nodded, wondering what she wanted. "I work for a modelling agency called 'Top Models' – you may have heard of it."

"No," he replied.

"Ah, well, we're looking for young, good-looking people like you to model top quality products for our clients." He looked puzzled. "Yes, like the photographs you see in the magazines. Here, let me show you some examples." He poured over the pictures with growing interest.

"Is there any money in it?" he asked.

"Oh, yes, lots of money, if your pictures help to sell the products." She smiled and he reciprocated. This could be just the thing, he thought to himself, easy money. She could see he was interested and there was no doubt in her mind that he would be a success – the minute she set eyes on him she knew. Before long, Marlon was the name on everyone's lips and a must-have at all the swankiest parties and events; his presence could mean the difference between success and failure for the host.

One of the many people Marlon met was Alan Wharla, an impresario with connections everywhere, who came across as friendly and good-natured. Alan had first seen Marlon in an advert for men's fragrance and was smitten. He was thrilled when Marlon turned up at his party. Over the weeks he courted Marlon, grooming him, making him feel special. Up close, he was even more attractive and, even better, young enough and inexperienced enough to be grateful for all the attention he was getting. Alan immediately took to him and they became friends. Marlon looked on him as an older brother and Alan became his mentor, guiding him through all the pitfalls that awaited a naive young man in such a cutthroat world. When he gauged the time was right, Alan seduced him, and Marlon was surprised to find that he had enjoyed the experience more than he did when having sex with women.

For six years, Alan and Marlon were inseparable. Alan's friends were put out; usually what happened was that Alan would find a new young man but, after a few weeks, would get bored and discard him without a qualm. This relationship was very different – if they did not know better, they would say he was in love. They waited, patiently, for the telltale signs that things were changing.

Marlon gazed at himself in the mirror; he was getting older. His skin was no longer translucent and a network of tiny wrinkles spread across his face. Younger men were beginning to take his place. There was nothing obvious that he could point to, exactly, and Alan was still very nice to him, attentive and clearly fond of him but, through tiny differences in his tone of voice, his expressions and the amount of attention that he paid him, Marlon knew Alan was changing towards him and that deep, fierce love was burning less brightly. Only the other day he had seen Alan cuddling a young

90

boy when he did not realise Marlon was nearby; Alan was gradually giving more and more attention to these nubile youngsters and Marlon was forced to submit to greater sexual humiliation to retain Alan's patronage and protection.

The thought of losing Alan filled Marlon with fear; he had been with Alan for so long, relied on him so much, he could not imagine any other life, could not imagine being let loose into an alien world that he was ill-equipped to navigate alone. He knew that Alan prized good looks above everything and that, without his good looks, he was worth nothing to him. He could not shake these fears from his mind – noticing the little slights and the preferential treatment that Alan was giving to some of the best looking teenage boys made it all much worse – and worst of all he was making mistakes around Alan.

Things came to a head when Marlon knocked at Alan's door and, instead of waiting for permission to enter as he normally would, walked straight in. Alan had been in the middle of talking to a young lad. "All right, Darren, you're a good boy, just the kind of boy I'm looking for. Come back and see me when you're ready." Alan smiled at Darren paternally, very much like he used to smile at Marlon. Darren smiled back and nodded. When he became aware of Marlon's presence he got flustered and struggled to put his clothes back on; Alan looked furious and Marlon knew he had made a terrible mistake, the kind he might not be able to rectify. Once Darren had left the room Alan turned on Marlon. "What the hell are you playing at, barging into my office like that?"

"I'm terribly sorry, Alan, I didn't mean to do it, I'd never knowingly do anything to upset you. I was preoccupied with the party – thinking about the planning – and I wanted to talk to you about it."

"Ah, yes, the party." Alan's expression softened. He grew thoughtful. Marlon was becoming a liability and he wondered what to do about him. "That reminds me, I'm meeting with Paul and Ian later. Why don't you join us and we can talk about it then?" Marlon nodded and left the office. Alan seemed to have let him off lightly, and he breathed a sigh of relief, but uncertainty still niggled at him.

91

You never knew with Alan, but there was nothing Marlon could do about it, he would just have to wait and see how things panned out.

In the afternoon, Marlon made his way to Alan's office; Paul and Ian were already there. They exchanged greetings. "We're going to the old pool house, Marlon, to have a look at the equipment for the party. It arrived very early and it's all wrapped up, so no one can guess what it is." Alan winked at Marlon and the two of them walked a bit behind the others. "Just like the old days, eh?" Alan put his arm around Marlon's shoulder; he was feeling sentimental and wishing that things did not have to change but, of course, they always did. As they neared the pool house door Alan moved forward a little. Marlon followed him in and, as he did so, Paul attacked him from behind with a baseball bat to the legs. He fell to his knees. Alan turned to Marlon and said, "I'm sorry it has to end like this, I truly am, but everyone's time comes eventually. I'll miss you, my boy." Without looking back, he paused to straighten his tie and walked out of the building.

With Alan gone, Paul and Ian could do as they pleased. They used the baseball bats to soften him up and then other, crueller methods to enter his body and have their way by whatever means they chose. They were having fun – all those years out in the wilderness after Marlon arrived, the new beautiful boy, the humiliation, the jealousy, the two of them thrown out on the scrap heap to make way for him – it was payback time. "Shut him up, Paul, for God's sake," Ian growled. "Do you want the whole world to hear him?" Paul looked around. "There, over there." Ian pointed to some rags in the corner. "Stuff those down his throat. Hurry up!"

"All right, all right. Who the hell do you think you are, bossing me about?"

Ian quickly diverted Paul's attention. "Over there, Paul, do you see that pole? Bring it over here. I know just what to do with that." Both men laughed. "See? Just the job to loosen him up inside – he's so tight I can't get in." Marlon's strangled screams hardly registered. They waited a while and then prodded him several times but got no reaction. "I reckon he's dead." Ian looked at Paul and they slipped out of their protective clothes, which they bundled up in plastic

92

bags, locked the door and hurried out; there was a lot to do before the party.

A CHRISTMAS SURPRISE

*by **Moyra MacKyan***

Kitty was sitting in her bedroom, deep in thought; she and her sister, Beth, were trying to decide what to get their family and friends. Kitty was determined to think of original presents – she did not want any socks, scarves or handkerchiefs creeping onto her list.

There was a knock on her door and Beth looked in. "How are you getting on?" she asked.

"Not very well," Kitty confessed. "It's really hard to think of things to get and I'm completely stuck."

"So am I. I think we'd probably find it easier if we were in the shopping mall, actually looking at stuff instead of just using our imaginations."

Kitty considered her sister's idea. "Yes, you're right. Let's ask mum if she'll drop us off at the shops on Saturday."

Satisfied with this plan, they walked out of Kitty's room, heading for the stairs. Once on the landing, they could hear their parents' voices coming from their bedroom; they were arguing. The girls crept as silently as they could till they stood next to the bedroom door but in such a position that, if anyone were to suddenly come out of the room and see them, it would look as if they were just about to go downstairs.

Their father was on his favourite rant. "Christmas presents are a complete waste of money and wrapping paper is a complete waste of trees."

"But, darling, it's such fun to see the pile of presents growing under the tree and to gather round to open the presents on Christmas morning, feeling them and trying to guess what's inside, but giving up because the excitement gets too much to bear, and there's nothing for it but to tear off the wrapping and see what's inside."

94

"But that's entirely my point. Why bother using wrapping paper; you can't salvage any of it to use again, it just gets thrown away, and most of the presents aren't worth having."

"That's not fair. When we give each other presents we're showing we care about and love each other and that we're buying something nice that we think the other person will like."

"Then why do people insist on buying me things that I don't like and don't want?"

"But you refuse to give anyone clues about what you would like so we all have to guess."

"Why should I have to give clues? You should all know me well enough to get me things I want."

"Oh, for heaven's sake, presents are part of Christmas, like sherry and mince pies. Instead of moaning, and being thoroughly ungrateful, you should show some appreciation for the efforts we've made."

"No, I won't! I don't like mince pies and I hate sherry. Why should I show appreciation when I'm unhappy. No one bothers trying to make me happy."

"Orrrrgghh. You're such a killjoy, Mike. It's the same every Christmas. I'm fed up and I'm going downstairs." The doorknob rattled violently and the door flew open as their mother marched out.

"Well, just to make things perfectly clear, I'm not buying anyone any Christmas presents." Dad shouted after her.

A few minutes later, their father came downstairs and put the kettle on, bringing a tray of tea and biscuits into the living room as a peace offering.

Neither their mother nor their father alluded to the subject of presents or wrapping paper again; nevertheless, the girls waited for their father to leave the room before asking their mother if she would take them to the mall so they could do their Christmas shopping.

It was the same every year. Ever since they could remember, their father had been like this; Christmas became tense, fraught, and miserable. Their mother put a brave face on it and tried to make it jolly, but there was an underlying unhappiness that

95

permeated the entire holiday. The girls did not understand what was wrong with their dad. Other dads seemed so cheerful; some of them even dressed up as Father Christmas. They wished he could be like them; after all, it only lasted a short time and then it was gone for a whole year.

The sisters were determined to ignore their father's unreasonable attitude and the mall made it easy for them to enjoy themselves by creating a truly wonderful experience; the magic began as soon as they walked through the doors. In the stairwell between the two central escalators rose a gigantic, real fir tree, full of baubles, garlands and lights, with a beautiful, life-size angel at the top; at the base of the tree stood a huge sleigh, stuffed full of brightly wrapped presents, with six life-like reindeers at the front, moving their heads and stamping their feet, with steam coming out of their nostrils; inside the sleigh sat a real Father Christmas, handing out gifts to all the small children.

The whole place was packed with shoppers weighed down by carrier bags full of festive treats and mysterious parcels wrapped in gold, silver and red foil. The Salvation Army was there, playing Christmas tunes, and a choir sang carols, their voices augmented by crowds joining in with great enthusiasm; it was an experience that Kitty and Beth would never forget. They visited every shop and, before very long, they, too, were weighed down with bags full of brilliant surprises to dazzle their friends and relatives, their Christmas spirits completely restored.

Three days before Christmas, Beth was on her way to her bedroom; she was surprised to see that the door of her parents' bedroom was closed. She could hear her father talking and hoped he was not having another row with her mother.

"Who's daddy's favourite doggie then, hmm?" Belle made a wuffing sound in response. "Yes, it's you, clever girl." Beth could hear rustling noises and then her father spoke again. "This is our secret, baby Belle. Daddy has to hide this in the box on top of his wardrobe, so no one sees it." More wuffing sounds.

Beth was surprised and perplexed. This seemed like a new development in the Christmas saga. Did it mean that dad had had a change of heart or maybe felt guilty? What had he put in the box –

96

was it a present for mum? She went to find Kitty to tell her of the curious conversation she had overheard. They needed to know what was in that box, so they decided to defy their father's strict orders not to touch his things and, when their parents were out, they fetched the big ladder from the garage and hauled it up the stairs. They leaned the ladder against the wardrobe and Beth climbed up, while Kitty held it steady. Kitty watched her sister as she moved the box towards her and opened the lid.

"Well, what is it, what's inside the box?" she called impatiently.

Beth slowly turned and looked down at her. "Nothing – there's nothing inside the box – it's empty."

"What? Come down and let me have a look." Kitty could not believe what Beth had said and needed to see it for herself, to confirm it with her own eyes. She climbed up and opened the lid. It was true, the box was empty. What on earth had been in it? Whatever it was, dad had outwitted them and they would not know until Christmas day whether he had changed his mind and bought mum a present or not.

It was a cold and frosty Christmas morning. Mum and dad were still in bed so Kitty took the opportunity to take another look at the pile of presents under the tree. She was desperately hoping that dad had slipped something under the heap but she turned away disappointed; it was all as before.

After the ritual of mince pies and sherry, they all settled round the tree. It was Beth's turn to hand them out; each person unwrapped their present to the accompaniment of suitable gasps and exclamations from the others. Beth picked up a big, floppy parcel which she had bought for her sister and, as she raised it up, she stopped and stared; there, on the carpet, lay a slim, elegant box, exquisitely wrapped, shining in the Christmas lights. Putting the floppy parcel down again, Beth picked up the box and, unable to speak, passed the gift to her mother who could see this was not something her daughters could have bought; it looked very expensive. She could not meet her husband's eyes as she delicately removed the wrapping paper and then stared at the embossed label on the box; it was one of the most famous jewellers

97

in London. She stood up and moved to the mirror to put it on, her hands trembling.

"Here, let me help you." Her husband was at her side, fastening the clasp round her neck. She stared at her reflection: a part of her could not believe what was happening. Gently turning her round to face him, he gazed into her eyes and whispered into her ear, "Happy Christmas, my darling."

Secret Sniper.

by **Mary McClarey**

Casualty had been frantic and she was late again. The heavy black crepe-soled shoes were dropped outside her door, ready to catch Anna's eye and encourage her to call in. Sweaty, fumbling fingers of both hands were needed as she struggled to free the tight stud securing the starched and scratchy nurse's collar, so she kicked her bedroom door open with her foot before beginning to unzip her uniform. Stubbing her toe, she groaned. Then she felt that gentle familiar pop where the nylon gave way to just one extra snag of pressure and 'Christ-the-night, this is all I need. Bloody ripped tights now and I haven't a clean black pair for tomorrow.' Grumpily kicking the door closed behind her, using her heel so as not to hurt the injured toe, she pulled aggressively at the zip running down from chin to knee and wriggled impatiently out of her dress.

Stepping out of the muddle of washed-out blue cotton fabric, she left it to join the other discarded clothes on the floor. 'Hurry, hurry,' she muttered, pulling the tights down, accidentally dragging knickers down to her knees at the same time. 'For God's sake, why don't they make them all one? You never can get the tights down without the pants coming too. Might have to go wild and free the night.' Then she had second thoughts. Even though it was summer, it was way too cold. She thought it would freeze the balls off a brass monkey, particularly one without underwear. Reminding herself that there weren't many brass monkeys hanging around in Belfast, and cackling out loud, she announced to the empty bedroom 'here's a clean pair. Bikini briefs they call 'em now. Never had a bikini, never left Ireland and it's never bikini weather here. Bit tight round the ol' tum. Never mind, have to do. Sure no one's going to see them anyway.'

Bending over to pull them up, with her back to the window She cried out a victorious 'Oh Yea' before standing up and pinging the elastic around the top of her leg, giving her backside a friendly slap of approval. Then, as she turned round, that's when she saw him. Staring straight at her through the wide clear window was the blackened face of a soldier, wearing a camouflage helmet. His rifle pointing straight at her bare belly button.

Maureen dropped onto her knees, hiding behind her unmade bed. She was getting used to dropping to the floor any time there was an army presence, or shooting, going on. She and her friends always watched TV sitting on the floor with their backs to the sofa now. It guarded them, they were told by friends who lived in the Falls, from any shattered glass which might fly in. It made them feel safe and secure. Mum and Dad couldn't understand why she preferred to sit on the floor now when she came home. She said it was just habit, although it was difficult to eat scrambled egg like that. Well, there she was, kneeling beside the collected debris of shoes, underwear and yesterday's black tights, in her too small knickers, beginning to see the funny side. Slowly, reality began to push its way to the front of her mind, making her forget the embarrassment of being caught undressed. Of course, she reckoned, it was just as likely that the soldier, based on the flat roof opposite her room, was not pointing the gun at her exposed flesh at all. He was probably keeping an eye on the whole hospital area. Still and all, she had felt exposed. "But not in a bad way," she reflected, "He wasn't some ol' letcher. He could be a bit of talent really."A knock on the door and her friend Anna walked in.

'What on earth, Mo?'

'Hi Anna. Soldier. On the roof.'

'Where? Him over there? You Eejit, he's been there for days. Jackie has a notion of him.   Thinks he's gorgeous, so she does.'

100

'Never noticed him before. Anyway, I'll be late for Frank if I don't get dressed.'

'You could go just as you are, that'd please him!'

'In these scruffy pants? You reckon?'

Anna pulled the curtains closed. Maureen was hugging her knees, showing no inclination to get up from behind the bed.'Anna, you know that time that bloke came to your door and then opened his coat and showed you his dick?'

'Yea.'

'Did it bother you? Did you feel bad?'

'Nah, I just looked at it, the wee dangly thing, and said "Och,catch yourself on."Then I   closed the door. That's probably what he did an' all.'

'What?'

'Catch himself on! Anyway, I'm away out now, enjoy yourself tonight, be good.'

Maureen dressed quickly, squeezing into her favourite outfit. A purple velvet all- in -one pantsuit with bell- bottoms. Then on went the platforms, completing, she hoped, the transformation from Frazzled Nurse to Beatnick Chick. Slicking on some pale lipstick and quickly drawing a black line of Kohl around her eyes, Maureen stood back and checked her image in the mirror. She thought she'd done a great job - she was especially pleased with the way the rings on the chain belt hid the bulge where the belly overstretched the knickers.

Her mind moved happily on to the next challenge-would he like what he saw tonight? Then, unexpectedly, was she dressing for him or the soldier? She knew she wouldn't tell him about the soldier, that would be her secret. Pulling the curtain back she looked across the rooftop. Jackie's favourite was still there. Noticing her, soldier Terry gave a grin and a wave. Maureen had a fair idea, and it didn't make her too unhappy either, that he had enjoyed watching her. She surprised herself by waving back. Maybe, she thought, I'll give Jackie a run for her money. But I'll never tell her.

True Friends.

by **Mary McClarey**

As soon as we heard the bad news, us girls got together to share our memories. I was quick to make sure they knew where I stood, and told them straight. 'I was always the closest to her, so I was. She was like a sister to me.' 'Yes, but remember,' Sue interrupted immediately, before there was time to hear what I had said acknowledged by the others, 'It was me she came to when she needed spiritual guidance.' And not intending to be left out - was she ever? Eileen got her spoke in straight away. 'Well, I've known her since she was knee high to a grasshopper. I'm almost family.'

Me, Sue and Eileen. Now we were all describing ourselves as being her very best friend. Of course we were. And how we vied for that pole position. Each of us thinking she should be Chief Comforter. We felt so sorry for her. Carmel,our dear old pal, abandoned by her husband.

It was actually one of Sue's churchy friends who told us first. They loved bad news. I always thought they took great pleasure in spreading tales of misfortune. Sue's lot liked to think about someone being dead whilst they were still here, shuffling along. But of course, Carmel wasn't dead, just unfortunate. Bereft, I think you could call it.

Straight away, Eileen and Sue said they'd come with me to meet up with her, although we all knew it was my idea. So anyway, I let them come, because I thought she'd need some serious supporting. Not a job for one person on their own. Looking back, I think you can safely say I was right on that count.

The four of us first met at nurse training, in Belfast,way back in the swinging sixties. Only it wasn't swinging in Northern Ireland. The pendulum seemed to have slowed its rhythm mid-ocean. By the time it reached the northern shores it was the seventies, and we only had the show bands in the dance halls. No Beatles or discotheques, not for us. And what with the Presbyterians making all the rules there was certainly no swinging, no free love nor even any cinema on a Sunday. Of course we did have lots of spare men - there were soldiers on every corner.

But here's the odd thing about Carmel. She'd up and left nursing years ago to become a freelance author. Silly woman,we'd all agreed, abandoning the good pension and the security just like that. And what sort of author had she turned out to be anyway? I heard it was just a couple of novels and a few poems published. Oh, and someone said she had done a wee talk in a bookshop somewhere - Foyles perhaps? Nothing much really, any of us could have done the same if we'd had time. That's all we had known about her until we heard of this tragic turn of events.

Anyway, we decided to make it a bit of a do,thinking it would surely lift her spirits. We could show her our photos, cheer her up to see the lovely grandchildren. Really, we agreed, it was the least we could do. Now I wonder why we bothered.

As you would expect with decent, hard - working women, we'd all changed a bit over the last forty years. Sue hadn't kept too good and since her second stroke her mind didn't seem all that clear. The stroke couldn't be blamed altogether though. She was always a bit thick, interfering when hearts were broken and offering unasked-for guidance. I remember her giving Carmel a dose of advice once on a boyfried who'd gone astray. 'He was a heathen, I never liked him, sure he had no religion in him at all. Then, to make matters worse 'I'll introduce you to my cousin Robbie, he's getting out of prison soon. He's only a political prisoner, no crime in it.' Carmel ignored that gem, thought she could do better. She might have had something there.

104

And Eileen? Well anyone would be a bit unattractive if they drank as much as she did. She was always wild for the men. Have I said she'd be there for us? Oh, true enough, Eileen had always been there, although not necessarily for us. She'd been right by the boys just as soon as she heard there was one going spare. In fact, once she was there just a wee while beforehand. She knew how much I liked him too. I never trusted her after that.

All things considered then, I was feeling pretty pleased with the way I'd preserved myself. No cancer anymore and only a bit of arthritis to bother me now and again. But of course the steroids are marvellous, plumping up my face, a wee bonus. They really do reduce the wrinkles. It gives me a calm expression, no one ever knows what I'm really thinking. Just as well as it turned out.

On the day in question I arrived at the hotel early, in time to choose a good firm seat positioned just across from the main entrance, where I could keep watch. Luckily Eileen and Sue were already at the bar so I motioned to them to bring me over a small sherry. I certainly wasn't intending to heave myself out of the chair when I'd just got settled. 'Gorgeous barman,' Eileen remarked when she brought my drink over. 'Quick with the service and lovely manners.' Thrice married herself, I remember wondering whether Eileen's opinion of men was all that reliable. And you could tell she'd been making good use of the Gorgeous to get a few down her. The lipstick had smudged a bit and that heavy mascara she favoured had worked its way down her cheeks. It was not unusual to see her like that and goodness, I remember thinking."Who minded how Eileen looked anyway?" 'Sure you're looking great Eileen. You're always so good with the make–up.' I'm not the kind of friend to look down on someone even if she isn't all that glamorous, not like some of our friends.

So there we were, speculating as we sipped, sitting in the Grand Hotel lobby."Will we recognise her?" I thought. "I bet she's let herself go a bit." I was expecting that, to be honest with you. 'Might she play the poverty card on us? Will she feel out of place in a smart place like this?' I remember Eileen asking. 'And I hear she

105

never takes a drink now. For heaven's sake,why not?' and then I just had to ask Sue 'Maybe she's found Jesus? You think that could be it? You know about these things, we'll leave her with you if she starts getting all preachy.' 'Or got cancer', Sue slurred in response, turning to me, a bit tactlessly I thought. Difficult speech, I could just make the words out, through the stroke-damaged muscles. 'You did have a bit of that Pat didn't you? No' a big deal really. You always had too much hair. I remember how you used to pluck away at the chin! But would chemo put Carmel off the drink? I'd say there's a lot more to cancer than you think.'

I changed the subject before my temper overwhelmed me, and that's not something I do. Charity has always been one of my virtues, anyone will tell you that. Turning to Eileen, filling in time really, getting bored with them both and keen to keep a bit of conversation going, I asked 'Maybe she's watching her figure? I think we all know the drink can pile the weight on, don't we?'

Perhaps I was just a tiny wee bit tactless there but anyway, Eileen wasn't having any of it. She stood up straight away. Her legs might have been a bit weak but her voice certainly rang strong across the foyer.'Just like your arthritic hip and no exercise eh, Pat? But Carmel? Watching her figure? She was always too skinny for my taste, never needed to watch it and no kids to stretch the belly either.' Holding her empty glass aloft like a trophy she continued 'I know all about it. Divorce. I always got the kids. No kids, no allowances, that'll be a real problem for her.' I watched Eileen walk across to the bar, red heels wobbling. Taxi to table shoes those were for sure. She never asked me did I want a refill either, only thinking of herself as usual.

So there you have it. Sue was telling me some tale about her many grandchildren, boring and difficult to follow, but that was what she liked to do so I was letting her. Keeping my eyes on the door with half an ear to Sue, I could drop the odd 'Really lovely kids,Sue.' or 'You must be so proud.' Without giving it too much attention.

No one who'd come in so far had looked the least bit like Carmel. My attention wandered and was caught by the glitter on a pair of Gucci sunglasses. Gucci are a bit brash for my taste, but I liked the way they were perched fashionably on a head of sunstreaked blond. That did look quite nice. I could always spot a bit of style. Another one of my strengths, everyone said so. I have really good taste. But as my eyes lingered, I felt my jaw dropping. I recognised that face. It was her, our friend. What a deceitful liar. She wasn't bereft at all, she actually looked quite well-to-do. Slender and expensively dressed. I watched as she briefly kissed and dismissed the good-looking man at her side. Just as he turned away, seeming reluctant to leave her, she raised her head and saw me staring. I could see the shock on her face as she recognised me. That's when I remembered - I'd never liked her at all.

Gone

by *Mary McClarey*

He's gone, my son, and left a mark.

A boy shaped space, which once

He'd filled with spice and sweat and heat.

Will time condemn his scent to fade?

Just as a fish slips through the reeds

disturbed, gone, but trace remaining.

Perhaps was real, or would one flicker

Still show a shimmering trail displayed?

When stoney wall and thorny hedge

Reveal a calf-shaped space

Does creature's snags of hair and muck,

Recall a boyhood churning?

For gone is never really gone

In life, all things keep moving

Sometimes the faces we love return,

While others just keep turning.

A Secret friend: Afrim

*by **David Rhys Shannon***

"Ho ho. Merry Christmas. Big Issue," Gheorghe adjusted his Father Christmas hat. Children were pointing at him laughing. He smiled back: Afrim had been right. The Welsh people have two Christmas's, he had said; to show their independence. Gheorghe had to dress up. It's very important to wish them a Merry Christmas, he had said; they'll love it. As he stood outside Swansea's shopping centre, he thought that his home seemed a million miles from here: A tiny village called Mogoş tucked away in a fold of the Apuseni Mountains. Christmas time in Romania was a distant memory.

Last December had been Gheorghe's first Christmas in Wales. This second one held mixed emotions for him. He shared the happiness of the local's celebrations: the joy on the young children's faces; smiling people laden with presents; much raucous singing of carols by good humoured, drunken young men with florid faces, fuelled by an abundance of alcohol. Much to Gheorghe's disgust, the young women too were drunk. When they pursed their lips, approaching him waving mistletoe about their heads, he'd make excuses and leave. His sisters would not behave this way.

Since July, home had been the hostel just off The Strand, run by the missionary's charity. It was a kindly place, food and basic accommodation provided. The usual rules: no drugs or alcohol; prayers twice a week. All residents had to be out between 9am-5pm (summer time) and 9am-4pm (winter time). Not bad, Gheorghe thought: better than Romania, especially in the cold winter months, no heating, family of ten in three rooms with a backyard outside, cold running water shared with their prize animals. But there was always Christmas. Christmas was special in Mogoş. Quietly he started humming his favourite carol, *"Top Tall Sky."* Instinctively, his free fingers mimed the intricate note sequence that the Torogoata demanded for accompaniment.

Strolling around the village with his five brothers on Christmas mornings, they always sang, *"Top Tall Sky"* with such gusto. It was invariably out of tune, but no one seemed to mind. The brothers would visit the humble houses, eating and drinking customary simple fare at every home. Gheorghe, being so adept at playing the Torogoata, the traditional wood wind instrument of the Balkans, had sore lips for days afterwards, from playing so many tunes.

He laughed softly, shifting his weight from one foot to the other, so as not to get cramp, his thoughts drifting back to his home. It was no fairy tale living in Mogoş; life could be hard.

His first Christmas abroad had been tinged with sadness. He'd missed the large snowflakes, gently falling, changing the pear shaped brown haystacks into huge iced cakes, giving the valley the appearance of a giant's larder; the scented smell of freshly-baked pound cake; Uncle Liviu dressed up as white-bearded Santa Claus - a family tradition; carollers' voices echoing in the village. All these added up to create an atmosphere around Christmas time at home, which belied the everyday struggle to survive. Then there was the food; the sacrificial pig; a Christmas feast, although parts of it lasted throughout the winter. His mother made sure of that. His father made the plum brandy that everyone drank, especially Uncle Liviu. He used to say, Ho ho ho is hard work, when you have to say it a thousand times! Adding, it makes you very thirsty too; the signal for his glass to be topped up, and everyone to laugh. He wished Afrim would laugh.

Afrim was a strange man. Being Albanian by birth was not strange: it was that sometimes he was very helpful, and other times he appeared to dislike Gheorghe intensely.

At the hostel, each dormitory had two sets of bunk beds complemented by two single beds. His room, Gheorghe's, was shared with Afrim, his brother Fatbardh, a fellow Romanian called loan, and two Poles whose names nobody could pronounce. They were simply known as "Top" and "Bottom," because of the bunks they occupied. When in residence, "Top" sprawled on the top bed and passed down the strong cheap vodka, bought from Afrim, to "Bottom" who was laid out on the bottom bunk. This practice continued through most of the evening until either the Poles were comatose, or one of the Sisters was heard approaching.

The Poles were gay Afrim told him. You can ask them, he said. Gheorghe did. The gay Poles laughed. It was a secret from the missionaries. Afrim told me, Gheorghe said. The Poles didn't seem amused. Next morning both Afrim's eyes were black.

The top bunk was a much-desired residence. One was becoming free this evening since Fatbardh, who weighed nearly one hundred and thirty kilos, was being transferred to another room with a stronger bed. Good riddance. Fatbardh by name, "Fat Bastard" by nature, Afrim had said. Even though he was the Albanian's brother, he insulted him, treating him with the utmost contempt. Fatbardh was just a big gentle bear, useless at most things, except crying. He cried most nights; some evenings too, sobbing for his home and his parents in the little village of Dragot, nestling in the Elbasan District of central Albania. The sleeping parents blissfully dreamed of their son's new-found happiness. Afrim had told them of a great new life they both had.

"Ho ho ho." The intonation didn't mirror the word's meaning. Gheorghe knew that. He also knew his Romanian accent detracted from this popular Welsh greeting. "Ho ho, Merry Christmas, Merry Christmas."

The crowds were dispersing as the shops started to close. In another twenty minutes, he would pack the magazines, fold his hat away, and finish for that day, and meet the Priest.

The Priest had told Gheorghe his conduct was exemplary, a shining beacon to all other residents. Secretly, the priest knew all the hostel's secrets. He knew the Poles drank every night. It's their way of coping with being gay, he thought. The priest knew that some residents were less than honest: some were, God forbid, Atheists!

111

But they were his motley flock, captured by the promises of a warm bed and full stomach. Gheorghe was honest and decent, to say nothing of his unswerving cheerfulness. That's why he'd assured Gheorghe he could have the top bunk tonight, and every other night. The news pleased Gheorghe, and made Afrim mad, much to the delight of the priest. He'd had to remind himself of Psalm 110: *"The LORD hath sworn, and will not repent; Thou art a priest for ever after the order of Melchizedek."*

Today, on this Welsh Christmas, Gheorghe had sold more copies of "The Big Issue" in the first five hours than he'd sold all last week. The shoppers were in good spirits, laughing at him and joking with him, but more importantly buying; or sometimes just giving him money. I'll thank Afrim, he thought. This was the second time his advice had really worked.

The first time was on St David's day. Afrim had told Gheorghe the history and importance of this Welsh Saint and the traditions he had bestowed on the religious Welsh.

Anxious not to offend the locals, at Afrim's suggestion, Gheorghe had dressed wearing the two traditional emblems of that day. On his left breast, he wore two brightly coloured Pansies, on his right, a small bunch of garlic; all obtained free of charge by Afrim. Gheorghe had trebled his takings. People stopped to stare, and then laughed. It was all in good humour. Being in a favourable mood, many of the Welsh felt generous enough to buy from him: one had even adorned him with an extra decoration: a yellow daffodil! But Afrim hadn't seemed pleased that night. In fact, he'd been angry, even when Gheorghe used the extra money to buy the trainers Afrim had stolen.

He'd buy Afrim a small gift, a token of appreciation, perhaps some tobacco.

"Excuse me, dearie." A tremulous old voice jolted Gheorghe out of his thoughts. He smiled as the old lady continued. "Don't mind me saying dear, but it's Easter bach. Easter, not Christmas." Gheorghe

112

nodded. "Just thought I'd let you know. Some foreigners see, they get it all mixed up, alright bach?"

"Thank you very much," he replied, smiling. "I have top bunk tonight."

That night he wallowed in the luxuriant sheep's blanket he'd brought from home. He could see the glint of the vodka bottle as it passed parallel to his head on-route to a thirsty Pole. The light fitting was dusty; one could not notice that from below, he thought, not that it's important. There was some graffiti, grittily scrawled in Albanian, besides him on the wall. He didn't understand it, but assumed Fatbardh had written it because he could make out Afrim's name, repeated many times; plus, there a doodle of a penis, entitled *"Afrim's brayn,"* written in Pidgin English.

Afrim lay glowering below on his single bed, plotting a final humiliation for that Romanian; Mr 'Nice Guy,' bastard, Gheorghe. May bank holiday was next month; he'd have to work out something really good by then.

Gheorghe had first fallen in love with the Torogoata In May 2009. Aged eighteen, he was of an age where he could be traditionally dressed for the occasion in the prerequisite headgear to adorn a male wedding guest. A black felt hat, fastened with white tassels, which were so arranged, they tumbled over the brim by a good half metre. A hand-woven waistcoat with intricate patterns of animals woven into a colourful background of coarse dyed sheep's wool, lay half hidden under a stiff cloth black jacket. His white breeches had bands of black braided wool around the waist. These were tucked into the smartest black clogs he could afford. Gheorghe had only worn the costume once, to his brother's wedding three years ago: a proud day for him, his brother and all the family.

The evening of the wedding, there was much celebrating and dancing. It was difficult not to dance to the haunting Romanian folk songs, played with such feeling upon the instruments of the Balkans. He'd stayed behind at the end of the evening to ask the soloist if he would teach him to play. The man, Alin Arcos, agreed.

113

One year's lessons for the exchange of one sheep and a dozen bottles of *Palincă de prune*, a traditional fruit brandy, a speciality of Gheorghe's father.

After twelve months Gheorghe was a natural virtuoso, so that even Alin was impressed. Gheorghe could become a professional in time, he'd said: if he had a genuine Torogoata, unlike the cheap Turkish import he'd practiced on, for that couldn't achieve the right pitch. But a good one cost the price of a small flock of sheep!

The family decided that they would club together enough money to get Gheorghe to the UK. There, he would earn enough to buy the instrument. This would be their passport out of poverty.

Today was that day. He'd earned more money than ever before in one single day. Gheorghe's delight was further enhanced via an E-bay message on his mobile. His bid of £850.50p had been the winning bid for a genuine Balkan Torogoata, which would be delivered from the Kentish antique shop by FedEx tomorrow.

Alin had told him when you buy the instrument, you have to live, eat, sleep, breathe it. It had to be your best friend; so, you needed to give it a name. Alin's Torogoata was called 'Puiu', after his cousin who'd lent him the money to buy it. The choice of name was easy for Gheorghe to decide: he would call his instrument 'Afrim'.

All he needed now was a case for the instrument, then he could return to Mogoş, ready for his new career. But a case cost money. He raised himself up on one elbow and looked down at the sleeping figure of Afrim. One more bright idea, he thought, that's all stupid Afrim needed to come up with; just one more idea my secret friend…

Aunties Secrets

*By **David Rhys Shannon***

Aunties have secrets; everyone knows that…

Aunties are special creatures. They have eccentric remedies to cure all household ills, especially those of young children. Clandestine concoctions, passed down from generations of greying geriatrics, served with a reassuring smile and that faint hint of liniment…

Then there's Aunties clothes, always interesting; mismatched, woolly and generally baggy, but somehow befitting and beguiling, on an Auntie….

When you visited, an Aunties dwelling, it was like a trip to an enchanted place set in another time. Faded photos of mysterious black and white Uncles were catalogued into ill-fitting wooden frames, which, like the now departed Uncles, no longer served any purpose. Old bottles juxtaposed jugs adorned with disinterested cows, rumoured once to hold milk. Both the cows and the jugs that is. On the mantelpiece sat the ubiquitous clock. Its ominous ticking penetrating briefly the periods of silence when an Auntie left the room. It made children jump when the Westminster chimes struck, but that was only occasionally, when someone had remembered to wind up the key…Somehow, as if by magic, it always chimed just before teatime.

And the food! cakes, tarts, and oh so wonderful trifles, adorned with one of Auntie's specialities. A single forlorn green glaced cherry: A neatly placed Jaffa Cake: Or a brazil nut, formerly a chocolate covered brazil, but now naked; maybe somehow, someone nibbled off the chocolate? Whatever the trifle it was always served warm. Whipped cream was banished; only fresh would do...

An Aunties crumb covered cardigan with its loosely hanging sleeves was an enchanter's robe. From hidden pockets, sweets magically appeared; toffees, mintoes, gums, boiled sweets, all sticky and covered with fluff; a treat for any covetous child. Naughty nephews gazed up heavenly at Aunties with ample bosoms, heaving with expectancy; whilst little nieces, like all small girls, gaped enviously at the splashing array of makeup painted on an Auntie's face.

At Christmas with Sherry stained lips, Aunties would sing with gusto, roaring out forgotten songs and rude rugby ditties, for this was the only time they sang. They remained resolutely silent for the rest of the year, fooling countless congregations by their ability to expertly mime any hymn that a chapel offered.

Some Aunties had a very dark secret indeed. They were the ones that were really Uncles!

Unavowed: Weeds in a Spanish Vase.

*by **David Rhys Shannon***

I saw you had fallen;

Not from grace, the sky or mountains.

Your head had just drooped, gently kissing

Ceramic lips, roughly shaped by Andalucían hands

In a time that is far from now.

The others stood tall for longer.

I felt taken by guilt, having seized you from your earthen bed

From which you cheekily sprang; waving your purple flowers

Insolently at the sun, daring it to shine steadily.

Now you're dying: a broken plant...

But, I loved you; I felt your beauty,

I embraced your faint floral scent.

You've lived your short life as a weed.

You died an object of beauty...

SECRET GARDEN

*by **Mary Thomas Levycky***

At the bottom of the formal garden was the wildflower area. Daniel asked Daddy if he could call it his secret garden, so that's what they called it. It was a sort of secret name, too. Daniel made little paths through it; he was the only one who knew where they went, weaving through the tall grasses. He loved the feel of their feathery heads, softly caressing his face and arms, his chubby little legs in their shorts, as they bent whichever way the breeze blew.

The wildflowers too, he loved. They each had a faintly different smell and whenever he stroked them their contours and shapes formed patterns in his head. Daddy told the gardener there must be no nettles or thistles in the secret garden though, because he didn't want anything to hurt the little boy.

In the middle of the secret garden Daddy had put three big rocks so he could sit down. All his hidden paths meandered towards them and Daniel liked to sit there and turn his face up to the sun, like a little flower himself. Sometimes he leaned on the tall rough rock, and sometimes he lay on the long flat one, which had a lovely smooth feeling. Daddy said it was called marble. The middle one was rounded at the edges and had lots of interesting grooves and hollows where he could put his fingers.

The garden was full of birds. Daniel often sat or lay on his rocks to listen to them. Some were sharp and shrill but the blackbird's song he recognised because its vibrato seemed to throb through his body right to his toes. When a bird suddenly flew above his head it made him laugh with surprise and happiness. In his secret garden, Daniel forgot he was blind.

118

SOONI

by *Mary Thomas Levycky*

Edith lay back on her pillows. Lydia watched her sleep for a moment before she kissed her fine silvery hair, then went to the door to ask a passing nurse to bring tea and cakes. She sat down again beside her Grandmother and gazed around the room. Not for the first time she thought how lucky Edith was, that she could afford a beautiful place like this. Two tall, elegant glazed doors let straight out onto the sweeping lawn which was dotted with ancient oaks and chestnuts. There were deer, squirrels and countless birds. Not to mention the damask sofa and chairs, the thick heavy curtains, the 24 hour care.

Edith awoke suddenly and said, 'I was dreaming about India.'
'Were you Grandma? I didn't know you knew anything about India?'
Edith looked amused. Her pale blue eyelids closed over her eyes and then opened wide.
'Of course I do. I lived there for nearly three years after the war'.
'Good Lord Grandma! I didn't know that!'
'Well you don't know everything'.

The maid arrived with the tea. Lydia poured and then helped Edith to sip a little. Edith went on, 'I used to go dancing during the war you know, in London. Roger Price-Worth and his crowd. All the young officers. That's how I met Amrit.' Edith smiled. Her eyelids fluttered. Ever since her fall she had become very fragile and now she looked every bit of her 96 years. She had also acquired the disconcerting habit of going to sleep briefly in the middle of a sentence. But her mind was fine.
'Amrit?' prompted Lydia, genuinely interested.
'Yes. He was so lovely. We used to dance all night. I put a little shiny brooch like a cat in his turban. He always wore it when we

120

went out.' Edith chuckled.

There was a long silence. Then she started talking again.

'It was horrid in London after the war, everything bombed and bleak. So Amrit arranged a job for me in India with his relatives, they were minor aristos, the Raja and Rani, and they wanted their daughters to grow up speaking proper English which I was going to teach them'.

Edith sighed. 'Oh they were gorgeous little girls! The eldest was a quiet, sweet thing, about four then, and there were little plump twins of two and a baby. I loved them and they loved me. We lived in a splendid house just outside Delhi with a beautiful garden. I remember how heavenly it smelt in the early morning and especially in the evening'.

Edith looked sad and plucked at her sheet. Lydia stroked her restless hand. 'Go on Grandma', she said.

'It didn't matter what we did you see, Amrit's family would not accept me'.

'What do you mean?' said Lydia.

'Getting married. We couldn't. We weren't allowed. Oh but we did so love each other. Amrit came over to visit all the time. They didn't mind that. We were happy.'

Lydia patted her hand. Edith slept for a few moments.

'Then it all changed of course, because then partition happened in 1947 and there were riots everywhere. Very frightening. So that's when everything got fucked up, as you would say.'

Lydia laughed. Then she said, 'what happened?'

'There was shouting and screaming, it was quite late at night. The ayah came rushing in and said the Raja and Rani had been killed! Their car had been set alight and they burned to death! There was a mob down at the back gate with knives and sticks, shouting and yelling. I was terrified! Then Sooni started screaming....'

'Who's Sooni?'

'The eldest girl, she was about six then, she ran out and down the drive.....she was trying to get to their car but it was burning. I

121

shrieked at her to come back and then Amrit arrived and told me to bring them all to the front and get in the car. He was going to take us away. I was crying and screaming "Sooni! Sooni!"

'God, it must have been awful. Horrible!'
' I can't tell you, Lydia!'
'Don't get so upset Grandma. Have some more tea.'
'But then, Amrit said, "Edith, you can't get her. It's too late. She's gone. We have to go now, or all the children will be dead and us too. Get the girls' boater hats, get in the back of the car and we have to go." I did what he said, I ran upstairs and got my hat, then I got theirs, and then I dashed passed the Rani's room and I suddenly thought – no – I'm not letting that mob have the Rani's things as well as her daughter so I scooped all her jewels across the top of her dressing table into my bag. I opened the drawers and got those too. There were a lot. Lucky I had a big bag. Then I ran downstairs and flung the girls in the back of the car he had brought. They didn't even cry. I asked him where we could go and he said the family had a summer house in Simla and we would go there, he had sent a message. He looked so grim. He usually looked so smart in his officer's uniform! He was covered in mess and blood. Oh dear.'
A tear appeared in the corner of her eye, which she wiped away with her thin fingers. The massive rings she always wore looked as if they would weigh too much for her to lift her hand.

Lydia was both spellbound and appalled. But whatever she felt, she just had to hear more. She helped Edith with a little fruit cake and another cup of tea. After a few minutes, the old lady continued:
'I said to Amrit, the people in Simla are expecting four girls and Sooni isn't here!' He was about to push me into the car. Then I saw this child, she was barefoot and ragged, hiding behind the pillar in front of the house, she was about six I suppose but a scrawny thing, tangly hair....anyway, I grabbed her thin little arm and shoved her into the car, plonked Sooni's hat on her and slammed the door. Amrit had already started the engine and we drove without the

lights on out the front gate, with all the rabble still screaming at the back...... all this only took a couple of minutes. I'm exhausted talking about it!'

'Poor Grandma!'

The old lady had another little rest. Then she galvanised herself. Lydia realised she had obviously planned to tell her this story.

'Amrit's plan was he would look like a chauffeur and we would look like a foreign family in our hats sitting in the back. We had the Raja's posh car. We drove and drove. We had to stop once or twice to have a wee but otherwise Amrit just drove. Nothing happened thank God, but there was fighting and rioting everywhere. Anyway, we reached the house in Simla and the ayah took the twins and the baby, and I took the ragged child to bathe her. She was a mess! Her eyes were blank. Heavens knows what she had been through. I washed her over and over again, washed her hair till it squeaked and then I cut it straight but left it long, then I plaited it when it was dry. I kept telling her she was Sooni. Her name was Sooni. I took her to my bed and she came with me as if she was in a dream. I felt so guilty about everything, the real Sooni herself, everything. Amrit thought I was bonkers but he just went with it all. During the night the new Sooni started to cry so I cuddled her and stroked her and she eventually went to sleep.'

'Amrit stayed with us for a week or so, then of course he had to return to his army duties. We were terrified of being parted, but one thing was for sure, said Amrit, after all this we weren't about to have any more nonsense about me being a governess and the wrong nationality and we would get married as soon as all this was over. He said we would live in America.'

'He came and went a lot over the next few months, he brought food and clothes for us all, we had a good bearer, and a cook and an ayah and I taught Sooni English and the bearer taught her proper Hindi which she didn't seem to know how to speak. Sooni and I became inseparable. The twins had each other and the baby had the ayah – that's how these things work you know. We got used to the way it was. Amrit and I were so happy. And when he

123

wasn't there Sooni and I talked and laughed and walked in the green hills. She was a very intelligent girl!' Edith's face was getting paler and paler, the shadows under her eyes becoming darker by the minute. But neither she nor Lydia could bring themselves to stop talking and listening.

'Then the unthinkable., the unthinkable,' Edith faltered.

'The unthinkable thing happened' she went on in a whisper.

'Don't talk about it if it's going to upset you Grandma,' said Lydia. Edith shook her head. 'I'm not dead yet', she said, with some of her usual spirit.

'Amrit was involved, or rather there was fighting, they were fighting each other on trains and hundreds of people were getting killed. And Amrit was killed', she finished in a whisper.

'Oh no!' cried Lydia, watching the tears roll down Edith's papery cheeks.

'Yes'.

'What did you do then?'

'A man came and told me Amrit had made arrangements. That's the kind of man he was.'

'I love him!' cried Lydia spontaneously. Her Grandma gave her a strangely conspiritorial smile.

'Then a friend of his collected me and took me to Bombay and I got on a ship. Amrit had arranged it all. This friend had already got the ticket. P&O.'

Lydia's mind was racing.

'But didn't you meet Grandpa on a ship? I thought it was from Rotterdam?'

'Yes. I did. We did go to Rotterdam, on the way back. Ships from Bombay often did.'

'So you met Grandpa on that ship? Just after Amrit was killed? Grandma?'

Edith took a deep breath.

'I told you Amrit arranged everything.'

'But not a marriage, surely?'

'No. Not that. But something'.

124

Lydia leapt up suddenly. She walked over to the mirror hanging by the window and looked at herself for a long moment. Then she slowly came back to the bed and picked up the photo Edith kept beside her all the time. A lovely picture of a beautiful woman and a gentle and kindly looking middle-aged man arm in arm. A fair man. A fair woman.

'Grandma. So did Grandpa have an Italian mother or not? So if he did how come he was so blonde?'

'Ah yes', said Edith, closing her eyes. There was a very long silence.

'So how come Mum and I have this black hair and these dark eyes? Grandma?' said Lydia, not knowing whether to laugh or cry.

'Apparently he did have some sort of Italian connection.'

'Ah come on!

'Grandpa was a friend of Amrit's and mine when we were in London you see', said Edith faintly.

'And....So what are you saying?'

Edith went on, 'Grandpa and Amrit always kept in touch. And Amrit knew Grandpa had been terribly wounded at the end of the war. It did irreparable damage. In the worst possible way for a man.' She hesitated. 'He knew Grandpa wanted a family and that he loved Amrit - and me', she added.

'So.....So....so.' ended Lydia, flatly. Edith lay back and closed her eyes.

'Don't speak to your Mother about it,' she said finally. ' You know what she's like. And her Conservative friends! She always said she took after Grandpa's glamorous Italian Mama. She liked that.'

'I don't know what to say,' said Lydia, half in tears, half laughing.

'Don't think Grandpa suffered!' said Edith, with some asperity. 'You know very well we had a lovely life and we were very well suited to each other. I loved Grandpa dearly'.

'You don't have to say that, I was there, I know!' Lydia sniffed.

Edith dozed for a moment.

'There's a magazine somewhere. I think it fell on the floor. Can

125

you get it, I want to show you something'.

Lydia looked on the floor. There was a Hallo magazine lying there. She looked at the cover. A splendid Indian marriage with all sorts of celebs appeared to be the main story. She sat on the edge of her grandmother's bed and read the headline aloud.

' "Celebrated Indian architect Lady Sooni Ragandath celebrates her grand-daughter's wedding to Count Eherd Shulz in Delhi and Geneva. Miss Aydita Ragandath and her bridesmaids ...."' Lydia stopped.

'Sooni? Do you mean THAT Sooni?'

'Yes. Worked out well, didn't it? Nobody every knew. Sooni didn't really remember anything from the time before. I certainly taught her not to'.

'And Aydita? Aydita? I've never heard that before, it's not.....'

'Yes, Sooni made it up. It's Edith in Hindi.'

'Of course!' Lydia said, laughing.

'Oh, how I love Sooni', said Edith.

'After the wedding she's coming to see me. I'd like you to meet her at the airport if you could, please darling?'

'So is that why you're telling me all this, now?'

'No. Well, not only. I wanted you to know where the money you're going to inherit came from, and I just wanted to tell you everything! I wanted to tell you about where you come from.' Her voice dropped so low Lydia had to lean forward to hear her. 'I want you to know Amrit through them. That's what I want'.

'Thank you Grandma', Lydia whispered. Then she tossed her shiny black hair over her shoulders and hugged and kissed old, beloved Edith, who held her hand briefly and dropped something small into it.

'Here's the cat brooch from his turban,' she said.

126

FLEXIBLE BORDERS

by **Mary Thomas Levycky**

Aidan watched him walk across the room, a tall, broad-shouldered man but pitifully thin. His cheeks under the high cheekbones were gaunt. Nevertheless, he saluted smartly. Aidan gestured for him to sit.

'I'm Lieutenant Tennant,' Aidan said, wincing as usual. 'I'm the Repatriation Officer. Tell me your name? How did you come to be a German POW?' He spoke in German.
'Piotr Petrovich Melinski, sir,' the soldier replied.
'Ah, you're Russian,' said Aidan in Russian. 'Sorry for speaking in German.'

'I am from Ukraine,' Piotr started.
'So we can arrange with our comrades in the Russian forces......'
'No!' interjected Piotr, 'no, I'm not returning to Russia.'
'Why not?'
'They will send me to the Gulag.'
'And why would they do that?'
'Because, sir, I fought with the Polish Army.'
'But you are Russian?'
'My Grandfather was Polish. Our village was Polish. The border changed.'
'I see,' said Aidan. 'But your papers are Russian?'
'I have no papers. Only German ones.'
'I see,' said Aidan, after a moment.

The chair creaked as Piotr shifted uneasily.
'Sir, they will truly kill me.'
'Where would you like to go then?' asked Aidan.
'To England,' Piotr said, 'where it's safe, there are laws.'
The young men looked at each other, one life in the other's

hands.

'What is your work?'

'I"m a steel worker. I am strong, sir'.

Their eyes met again.

'And 3 years in the POW camp? You were well treated?'

Piotr snorted derisively. 'You don't want to know,' he said.

Aidan wrote a note, then stood up. Piotr followed suit, heart thudding. Aidan shook his hand and said, ' You're a brave man. I've written that I'm not able to determine your nationality. So you can go to England as a refugee.'

Their eyes held briefly with unspoken emotion, then Piotr smiled.

A STORY OF GUILT AND PAIN

by *Mary Thomas Levycky*

It was the last night of our hard working, week-long show at the World Travel Market at London's Olympia. We were equally elated as exhausted by the time we had closed our small stand down, changed into our glad rags and gone on to the Grand Finale Dinner and Dance.

My boss Joe Mundell-Brown, he of the famous Beta World group of travel companies, and myself always took a stand at the World Travel Market, otherwise known as the WTM. Together we ran a two-person business called The Travel Community, supplying big firms like Ford with the details of ground operators in many countries, who could run business meetings and incentive programmes for their most successful employees. We published a directory containing all our operators' details from around the world with page long descriptions of what their different countries could offer, from whale watching to pony trekking to beer festivals and we did a lot of research, which involved travelling, feasting and raising our glasses worldwide.

It was a fiendishly clever idea and right on trend thirty years ago, when incentive rewards to employees were all the rage. We featured 160 operators in around 120 countries, and had good relationships with all of them; some of them were with us on that evening.

Mr and Mrs Rajid, as always, had come from Delhi for the final Saturday. Mr Rajid never travelled without Mrs Rajid: they were a matching pair. Short, sweet, and rounded they gleamed, he with his shiny black patent leather shoes, and she with her shimmering saris. Takis Hajimikalides from Cyprus, also a regular, and his Swedish mate Carl Something were there, and the lovely Miriam

Sladic from Yugoslavia who was, very sadly, later killed in Sarajevo. We had a charming and erudite new member from Yemen I remember; I had a fascinating talk with him about the ancient towns and ruins he had included in his programme, and we decided either Joe or I should visit as soon as possible - hopefully me. And of course our good friends Gunte Hartsmann from Amsterdam and Russell McClaren from Scotland were there, comrades-in-arms and always ready for a party.

We left the big Event Hall around midnight and straggled back to our hotel. It was cold, it was November, but we were feeling no pain as we walked the few minutes to the hotel bar and reassembled there in high spirits, whereupon Mr Rajid surprised us all by ordering quantities of Moet et Chandon and insisting we raised a glass or two in a toast to his first grandson Javit. This we did with alacrity. We were full of good cheer that night, laughing and larking about; even Mrs Rajid giggled over her orange juice and kissed me on both cheeks.

Eventually the Rajids, my new Yemeni friend and most of the others decided enough was enough and went to their rooms; a lot of them had long journeys home in the morning. Gunte, Russell and I were left with two full bottles of champagne which had miraculously appeared the way these things do on occasions like this. Then Gunte unfortunately threw up in the gents: admittedly he had been to an early drinks party at the WTM Nederlands stand, so he had been imbibing for at least two hours longer, and twice as heavily no doubt, than the rest of us.

Russell and I were left sitting by ourselves in the muted lights of the bar. The staff lowered the music and left us to it. I could see Russell was half sloshed but that wasn't enough to explain the distinct   distress I could see in his eyes. We were sitting close together on a leather bench; I had my arm along it and Russell reached up and grabbed my fingers.

'What's the matter Russell?' I asked him, puzzled.

130

He sighed but hung on to my fingers in a hot and sticky grasp. He was a great looking man, tall and chunky, with red-brown hair tied back in a pony tail. He ran popular adventure programmes based in Inverness, where guests could be accommodated in yurts or castles. Yurts are not for me; four years earlier I had swanned around at his glamorous castle "taster weekend" which is when I had got to know him.

'It's a bad day for me', he whispered. He leaned his head back on the bench.
'Why?' I whispered back.
'I've never told anybody'
'Well..... you don't need to now'
'No, I do. I want to'.
'Russell,' I said, 'You're really drunk, let's talk in the morning'
'But it's the anniversary. It's today. November the 24th'.
'Oh.' I took a sip of my champagne. 'Alright then. Tell me.'

'I'm not Scottish', he said after a long pause.
'Really?' I was very surprised, especially because his voice had a soft, Highland burr.
'No', he went on, pressing his back restlessly against the bench, 'I was born in New Zealand. In a small town, where it was all farming and sheep and everyone knew everyone....'
I was nonplussed. I looked up at him and saw there were tears in the corners of his eyes. He kept fiddling with my fingers. I pulled them away.
'Sorry'
'It's okay"
He sighed again, deeply.
'Look, it's two o'clock in the morning, maybe we should......'
'No,' he said, urgently, 'no, I want to tell you',
I took another deep swig of my now slightly warm champagne. Have you ever gone off champagne? I was fast doing so.

Russell suddenly slumped forward on the seat with his head in his hands. He spoke in a very low voice.

'We all knew each other in this little town'.
He cleared his throat. 'We all went to school together. I was a tough kid, my parents and my older brothers ran a sheep farm, we were outdoors kids'.
His voice tailed away. He looked straight at me. I could see his brown eyes now swimming in tears.

'I got in a fight with another kid in the playground at school and I hit him. I hit him hard and a lot and he fell down. The trouble is', he breathed deeply, 'the trouble is he didn't get up again. He was dead. I killed him'.

'NO!'

'Yes. I was nine. It all went to court. My parents sold up, we moved away but it wasn't enough, it was in the papers; my brothers said it ruined their lives because Dad sold our farm. He moved Mum and me and him to Scotland. He changed our name'.
He took a deep shuddering breath.

'McClaren was his mother's name....'

I put my arms around him and rocked him back and forth. He was sobbing, drunkenly and uncontrollably. The waiters wanting to clear the bar came in but left again discreetly. He pulled himself together eventually. He asked me never to tell his secret but it has haunted me for 30 years.

So now it can be told. Because last week I heard that he had died, still unmarried, not quite 60. Poor, beautiful, guilty Russell. Maybe it was his secret that killed him.

The Plymouth Writers Group
2017 Short Story Competition Winners

CAP IN HAND

by *Douglas Bruton*
(First Place Winner)

You ever knowed someone who's mam died and they was all broken like glass inside and they was your best friend ever? I din't know what to say or what to do and so I just looked at Carl, looking sad as wet sunsets or dead kittens, and being just as silent, and one hand on his shoulder and not sure that was ok to do.

She wasn't sick, his mam, leastways not so far as anyone knowed. She just died. Sudden as thunderclaps and no grey sky warning before it and no sparking flash-bulb light. Doctors said her heart just stopped and they said it can do that sometimes and not ever start again. And Carl swore hard as any man, all his words like thrown stones and all of 'em thrown 'gainst God and doctors and even his da. And 'fuck' and 'shit' and 'bastard', he said. Over and over again. And I told him to just let it out, like a poison released, and it wasn't never no sin to be doing like Carl was doing, I thought, not even though he was doing it in front of the church.

The minister came out to see what all the commotion was and his face was red as wasp stings and he was holding his fist up to hammer the blaspheming air. When he saw it was Carl, well, I think he understood, and he let fall his slack fist and he said 'There now,' and 'It's you is it?' and he asked us if we wanted to come gentle inside.

Carl shook his head and turned away and I turned away with him. The minister called to our backs, saying as how the door to God's house was always open. When we was ready, he said, anytime, day or night, and he blessed us in God's holy name. And Carl said all his best swear words again, saying 'em under his breath this time so only God and me could hear 'em.

We din't plan it or nothing. Not nohow. We just decided there and then to go, not knowing the place we'd go to or for how long, but knowing we had to get away and be by ourselves for a while.

We stopped off at my house and I picked up a bedroll and some apples and a leg of pork that'd been cooked and was cold

134

and mam'd said was for tea and then for sandwiches for the rest of the week. She'd be mad as a shook bag of ferrets when she found out, but it din't matter none to me, not with Carl the way he was and his mam waiting to be laid in the ground.

Then with the pork and the apples and the bedroll we just left, me and Carl. There wasn't hardly no words 'tween us and there din't need to be. We just walked up out of the town, the pull of the hill like something holding us back but not holding tight enough, and we kept on walking and not ever looking to the town we'd left behind.

The day was still and warm, and Carl beside me so close I could hear his breath catching; and my own heart drumming in my ears, I could hear that, too, and birds getting it all wrong and thinking this was a day like any other day and a day to be singing in.

We stepped off the road as soon as we could and headed into the trees, walking through deep ferns and wild garlic, and sticks breaking sharp like gunfire under our feet. It was cool in there, as cool as church stone, and the sky was in bits 'tween the trees and we walked till we was nowhere and till we was out of breath and out of the will to walk more. And we just sat down beside each other, sitting on a old fallen log with the sound of running water playing like music somewhere over our shoulder and the smell of Sweet Flag hanging all about, and Carl sucked air and blowed it out again, and I did, too, and it was like the weight of everything was in that moment we'd been brought to.

I wanted to say something then. I wanted it to be like in a movie and I'd have something important to say, something simple and clever both at the same time, something that'd make sense of where we was and what we was about. I wanted to make a small speech that'd stay with us forever after and we'd always be friends no matter what the world threw at us – cos the world could not throw anything worse than this, I thought, not anything worse than Carl's mam's heart stopping and never starting again. I wanted to say something.

But all I had was sorry, sorry for Carl's mam, but sorriest for Carl. So I said just that, said I was sorry and real sorry and sorry

135

right down to my boots. And Carl started crying – which the occasion told me was alright and sometimes crying ain't just for girls like people say it is. I put my arm round Carl and I held him tight as not letting go and he just cried hisself down to quiet and to sob and I din't have more to say to him.

Sitting like that, all still and near to silent, well it was like we slowly became invisible and a nat'ral part of the forest. It was like time stopped, or slowed at least, and nothing mattered 'cept me holding onto Carl and Carl holding onto me. And we might have stayed like that forever and it would have been enough – like the last frame in a movie and the music playing quiet and dwindling, and the picture fades slow to black and the credits come up in silence.

Then suddenly this glassy eyed red-flame squirrel just ran under our feet, skittering through last year's fallen leaves, and it stopped to look at us and to get a sense of everything, sitting up straight and it's tail curled into a question mark at its back. And Carl and me just looked at the squirrel what was looking right back at us, and bits of sunlight making rare gold on the forest floor, and me and Carl still holding to each other. And like that I reckon as it was better than any church and I could hear the voice of the minister saying soft as whispers that the door was always open, anytime, day or night. And I felt something then, and I think Carl felt it too, and God was there, I swear it, in that moment, sure as eggs, there with His cap in hand and saying He was sorry, too.

Wind Song

by **Sheila Blackburn**
(Second Place Winner)

When the wind screams from the sea, it flings the gulls like rag toys and makes the windows sticky with salt. The brave trees stoop and turn away, branches teased to spiked quiffs. The winter wind sings a bitter song, a harsh song, abrasive and demanding.

This is home now. The hebes and sturdy evergreens I planted in the early days grow strong and confident. Defiant against the song of the wind. Hardy fuchsias finger at the shelter of thick stone walls and the sleepy horses nod at the fence for peppermints and apples.

Spring-time winds soothe, but gust unexpectedly; they are the high and low notes of a whole symphony. The summer breezes have a liquid melody and in autumn, the wind tugs and bumps along with a strong bass note.
This is home. My home until the wind sings a very different song.

"There's lovely!"
Mrs Griffiths straightens, pulls at her corsetry and steps back to admire our seasonal arrangement. An unlikely couple, we have become the mainstay of the church flower rota. She doesn't care for my choice of hair-dyes; she wears her distaste as openly as her plain jumpers and sensible shoes. But I pose no threat; my diligence and reliability suit her and she has become a staunch ally.

Later, I plan to take more home-made pickles to be sold in the corner shop. Dewi Jones will brew a welcome pot of tea and twinkle over his half-moon glasses. He has reinvented and diversified – as we all must – with an eye on the tourist trade and a steely determination that is open to modern ridicule.
I find it inspiring.
"Never give up." Dewi clings to his business with the tenacity of

137

lichen on the windy cliff-faces. The fixed belief that I have had since first I came here…

Now, a crisp-cold December evening skitters tiny frost-sparks into the shop as I shoulder open the door and heave my produce onto the counter. Another cheerful jangling of the bell when I push the dark-cold back into the street. Dewi is already reaching for the kettle.

"It'll be a sharp one tonight," he beams and peers into the box. "The wind has dropped – there's maybe snow on the way."
He smiles approvingly at the red bows and holly sprigs I added to the jars, happily arranges them on a display with local wintry-greeting cards.

"The roads will be impassable!" His is a cheerful pessimism. "The gritters won't get this far – we'll be cut off…"

This *has* been my home for some years. Yet I have only just arrived. Being accepted takes time; it brings trust, but it is always tinged with reluctance.
I have trust, too. But mine is tainted with something else. The friendship I want and offer always carries a deeper truth, like a betrayal.
"There now, you'll have one of Maia's mince-pies?"

Tea and mince-pies and gossip are what I have earned over the years. Youthful willingness traded for cosy familiarity. I have come a long way to be here. The achievement is to be celebrated. But it comes at a cost. I carry it close – smile and say very little.

"Mind how you go." His words and the jangly bell carry me back out into the winter streets, where the wind holds its breath. Waiting. We are all waiting.
The huddled cottages are warm with window lights and sparkling trees; the night sky arcs and turns and the steel-white star-eyes are

138

piercing, - searching out the darkest secrets.
My boots beat a muffled rhythm along the empty road to sagging gate and
holly-wreathed front door.

This is my home now. Scent of cinnamon, glowing log-fire and a small tree ready to shed its needles. My old dog thumps his tail on the floor.

I heat some soup and take a tray to the fireside. So much warmth is soothing, but the agitation is never far away. Restless, I move around the room, touching things, wishing for the wind to sing again, to bring what it will.

Two travellers on the road tonight, looking for a place to stay, looking for a land-line when their mobile signal has failed. The knocking at the door startles me, brings back the old fears that I would have buried all that time ago on another night as clear and dark as this.
At the sound of strange voices, the old dog stirs from his grumbling sleep and frets at their feet. But these are not my persecutors. *They* will come, one day, for their justice. Perhaps I might lack the will to let *them* in.

But tonight, I open to a city couple, road-weary and lost. He is unshaven and in a long thin coat that flaps at his heels. The girl is diet- frail and vulnerable in clothes the elements mock and seer right through. And tonight, my compassion brings them in to a cheerful fire, to a welcome hot drink and to a phone call to the local hotel.

This is my compassion. But it is a short-lived, easy thing. It is given and they are gone - back on their wind-quiet winter journey.

Tonight, my compassion is simple; it has no struggle with things that are hard and final. I let myself be swallowed into the depths of the fire-side chair and the dog settles at my feet with a simple, unconditional love. Would that it was always so.

One day the wind will take all the compassion and love I have and fling it back in my face.   And the song will reach a just and triumphant crescendo.

I allow myself to be lost in thought…dare to reach into memories… How he walked into my life when the winter wind moaned long and low. He brought me calm and understanding and a little green pot plant with a red ribbon bow. In a short time, I let him in and let myself think he could give me love, where there had been no love before.

He came with so little, wanted little, thought to take nothing. He was gone when the late winter winds blew themselves to a haunting memory. Thought to leave so very little of himself for me. Not thinking, nor backward-looking, he never knew how much he truly left… A sweet, new song, stirring within.

My tiny stranger; a sense of shame, of foolishness, of trust too freely given. Of love that rose and fell on the wind.

No need to tell. Nobody to hear. - The new song, stirring, taking shape.

Stirring, humming softly, but not strong enough to hold its own life-beat.

I lost my child when the late summer breezes came to whisper at the smallness and the hugeness of it all. Nobody knew. Nobody heard. Nobody came.

I worked in a corner of the garden and at night, while the quiet stars watched and only the wind-song mourned, I wrapped her in a white sheet and carried her easily to where the apple tree branches creaked and pointed. I covered her with earth and a bag full of spring bulbs. It was only then that her song ended.

I stayed with her at the house until two seasons of bulbs had grown and bloomed and faded away. But then when the late spring winds had flattened the withered brown flowers, I sold to a young family who could unknowingly share their easy happiness near her.
And then I followed the wind here, where it can roam and sing freely.
Here is home. Here is where I shall stay. For now...

This night, I lie awake and think of Christmas and the kind invitations that mean I can choose not to be alone.
I lie awake and think of the city-wise travellers, in a hotel that will be no more than a basic comfort on their journey.

I lie awake and think of Spring and new life - and all the old worries come rushing and crowding in...
 Will it be *this* Spring that the wind turns? When they finally dig the furthest corner of the old garden? And make their find? And think they have uncovered a truth?
Tonight, there is no wind, but I hear the horror, the gasps, the words of their disbelief.
And where will acceptance be then? Compassion? Who will understand my special song?
Tonight, I lie awake on my own journey. I have arrived and am at home – but I will not stay. I cannot stay.

And tonight, there is no wind-song to whine or scream. Tonight, my own breathing moves the cold air with a haunting song of fear.
I lie here and wait for the wind.
It will be a wind that gnaws and worries and will not rest until the whole song is over.

Bycatch

by **Grant Price**
(Third Place, Highly Commended)

The Captain was lying on his bunk when the deck chief appeared in the doorway and told him there was a situation upstairs. His beard was soaked through with rainwater. The Captain put on his oilskin and followed the chief out onto the deck. The seiner was rolling hard on the waves. It was the type of cold that had a man pinching the meat on his cheeks to keep the blood flowing. The boys were standing by the roller at the back of the boat, backs turned and hoods up. They were ankle-deep in dead sockeye and peering over the stern.

'What's the hassle?' the Captain asked as he and the chief joined the pair of them. The boys didn't take their eyes off the water.

'Something in the net,' shouted one. He was an inbreaker, new to the seiner and not yet old enough to have reached his third decade. The Captain liked the boy. He was quick to learn and impressed without making a show of it.

The senior deckhand grunted. 'Something big.' The rain rolled off his orange oilskin. He pointed. 'Over there. Tangled up proper.'

The Captain narrowed his eyes and looked. He'd ordered the boys to gather the net in before it became too choppy. It was usually a quick job to pull it in with the drum, but not if a dolphin or a small whale had strayed into the seine and was trying to thrash its way loose. He watched the surface of the sea for the foamy spot, but saw only the rain lashing down.

'Nothing on the surface.'

'Went below a minute ago,' said the chief. 'Then I came for you.' There was a tone in his voice that the Captain couldn't place. He was gripping the coaming with both hands.

The four men waited in silence. The seiner rose and fell almost like it was breathing. The net dropped down from the roller and disappeared into the ocean. The senior deckhand coughed. The chief adjusted his hood and wiped at his eyes with a dirty palm.

'What did you see, boys?' asked the Captain. None of the men answered. The wind started to whip itself into a fury.

Then the inbreaker yelped and pointed. They looked. A form flailed in the water several metres away from the stern. The net held it fast. A tail quivered and disturbed the glassy grey surface. The Captain's relief was spoiled by a touch of regret. A dolphin. Unfortunate, but it was easier to dispose of than a whale.

'Reel her in, boys,' he ordered. The senior deckhand grabbed the slick rope and pulled. The net began to retract and hug the coiler. The inbreaker busied himself with the fish that slopped over the roller and hung suspended in the net. He clutched one in a practised hand and drove a spike into its hindbrain. The fins flared for a moment and then the fish fell still. He dropped it on the deck and moved to the next one. The bright orange handle burned in the Captain's eyes.

'That's right,' he said, encouraging the boy. 'Quick as you can. The storm will be on us soon enough.' The inbreaker nodded and kept on sticking. His mouth was a pencil scratch on bone. He needed a hot drink and a rest. Once the dolphin was out of the net, they could all get below deck.

'Get the gaff hooks ready,' called the chief, leaning over the stern. The Captain fetched them himself and handed one to the inbreaker. The senior deckhand made ready with the rope. The inbreaker wiped his spike and clipped it to his belt. He and the Captain joined the chief.

'Gone below again,' he shouted. 'Once it hits the surface, get it with the gaffs. Then we'll drag it in.' He held his hand up, ready with the signal. Behind them, the senior deckhand counted the seconds. The rain beat against their oilskins. The Captain blew through his nose.

The water parted and the tail smacked against the surface. The Captain held the gaff aloft, ready to lunge.

Then a pair of arms appeared.

Fingers poked through the holes of the net.

An osseous head crested the wave and stared up at the men.

The inbreaker screamed and threw the gaff into the water. The chief's hand fell to his side. The senior deckhand pulled hard on the

143

rope and the net retracted over the roller. The Captain turned and called for him to stop, but the sound was snatched away on the wind. The deckhand gave a final heave. Something slid over the top of the roller and slapped onto the fish-laden deck.

The men jumped back and pressed themselves against the sides of the seiner. The shape twisted in the net and tried to pull the fibres apart with knotty bluish fingers. The tail sent sockeye skidding towards the drum. It flipped itself over onto its back. Blood poured from underneath one of its arms and mixed with the water on the deck. Then it lay still.

Clutching his gaff hook, the Captain edged closer until he could see the face.

'Don't go near it,' shouted the chief. He was holding onto the inbreaker's oilskin.

A pair of fluid black eyes locked with the Captain's. The form had an enlarged forehead, nose and jaw. It opened and closed a wide-set, lipless mouth, but no sound emerged. Two rows of teeth stood out like broken glass.

The Captain turned the gaff hook over in his hands and held it out, wooden end first, towards the form. The blue fingers stretched and wrapped themselves around the wood. There was strength in the grip. The eyes continued to hold his gaze. The blood began to pool near the top of its tail. The Captain stood, legs glued to the deck of the bobbing seiner.

It let go of the gaff. Slowly, the other men approached and formed a circle around it.

'Captain?' asked the senior deckhand. His voice sounded as though it had been cracked in half and taped back together.

'I don't know,' said the Captain.

Then it lunged. The bony hands found the deck chief's ankle and yanked the man off his feet. His skull struck the body of a sockeye and the breath exploded from his body. Jagged teeth pierced the fabric and buried itself in the chief's flesh. The Captain bellowed and brought the gaff handle down hard on the tail, but the form refused to let go. The senior deckhand dropped to his knees and tried to prise its jaw apart. The tail thudded against the wooden boards.

144

Before the Captain could strike it again, the inbreaker dived past him and drove the orange-handled spike again and again into the back of its neck. The form trembled and its eyes froze solid. The tail stopped moving. The senior deckhand opened the jaws and the chief pulled his mangled ankle free with a cry. The Captain dragged him across the deck to the drum and told the chief to press down on the wound.

'Help me,' called the inbreaker. He and the senior deckhand cut the net off the roller and wrapped it around the body as best they could. Then the inbreaker grabbed the wrists. The deckhand took the tail. They lifted it to the edge of the seiner.

There was a splash. The two deckhands looked over the side before sinking to the floor. The chief moaned and clutched at his ankle. The Captain stared at the roller and the tattered remains of the seine.

And the men were alone.

Detroit

*by **Erik Lofroth***
(Fourth Place, Highly Commended)

'There's bacon and eggs if you want it.' She gestures towards the stove.

The man pulls out a chair. 'I'll just have coffee.' His cigarettes are on the table. He flicks a finger at the bottom of the pack, bringing one out, and lights it. The ashtray has been emptied but not cleaned. He places the lighter on top of the pack, then straightens it. 'Listen, Lauren,' he says. 'About last night.'

'Don't.' She holds out the frying pan. 'You sure you don't want any?' As he waves his cigarette in dismissal, she empties the contents in the trash. 'Eat up,' she tells the boy.

His protest is weak. 'Aw, Mom.'

She ignores it. Her elbow sticks out at a sharp angle as she dumps the frying pan in the sink. It sizzles.

The man pulls on his cigarette. 'You know you don't have to go through with it. We'd manage.'

'That's what his father said.' Her shoulder indicates the boy. She keeps her back to the table, scrubbing at the pan. 'A month of dirty diapers and broken sleep and he was gone.' The frying pan hits the side of the sink. She rinses it off and gives it a quick dab with a dishcloth before returning it to the stove.

The kid's head is bent forward, inches from the cereal he has hardly touched. 'You're not my dad,' he mumbles.

Unsure of his meaning, the man hesitates. 'I am for now,' he says. It seems a safe enough claim. He taps his cigarette against the ashtray. Coffee, he thinks. He puts his hands on the table to push himself up.

But Lauren is ahead of him — she has finished clearing up and pours them both a cup. 'Tyler will have to stay home,' she instructs him. 'I may not be out in time to pick him up from school.' Some coffee spills as she hands him his. 'There's leftover pizza in the fridge. There should be enough for you both.' She unties her

146

apron and drops it over a chair.

'Will you be able to drive after they're done?'

'Can't see why not.'

They sip at their coffee in silence. He stubs out his cigarette, lights another.

'Remember the lilacs?' he asks.

She doesn't.

'Never mind,' he says. 'You'd better be on your way.' He empties his cup and takes it over to the sink, along with the ashtray.

She joins him. 'A hug?'

He holds her. Over her shoulder he can see Tyler. The kid is looking away.

'If you should change ...'

She places a finger on his lips and frees herself to go and get her coat. Passing the boy, she gives him a sideways cuddle. 'See you tonight,' she says. And she is gone.

The man spends the rest of the morning tidying up. He strips the beds, theirs and Tyler's, hangs the sheets out the window, turns the mattresses over. He gathers Lauren's clothes, but not certain precisely where they go leaves them on a chair. Unhappy with the result, he transfers them to another chair, folding each item to form a neat pile. Tyler, who must have trashed his cereal as soon as there was no one watching, stays in the kitchen with a coloring book and a set of felt-tip pens. Had Lauren told him to? In it are pictures of spacecraft, robots, aliens. The man hears him fire a gun. 'Pow! Pow! Pow!' When he looks in on him, he sees him point a pen at the roach motel by the stove. 'They check in,' he whispers. 'They check in ...' He bends his head to the right for a better aim. 'Pow! Pow! Pow! Pow! You're dead.'

'You can't read yet, can you?' asks the man.

'Some.' The kid goes on firing.

When Lauren brought him home in the spring, she'd made no mention of Tyler. Had he taken even a casual look around, he would have seen signs of the boy everywhere, but he didn't — in two days, they hardly left her bed. In fact, she didn't refer to him until she had to collect him on the Sunday. 'He's been with his granny,' were her words. She'd wanted a weekend to herself.

148

Seeing that he'd stayed on, it had been the only one. How many had there been before him?

'Where does your granny live?' he asks.

The kid has his nose in the book. Is he nearsighted? 'On the farm.' He uncaps a black pen for the robot's handgun.

'Nearby?'

Tyler shakes his head. 'They have chickens.'

He should have found out from Lauren.

Deciding that the sheets have aired long enough, he makes the beds before he proceeds to sort out his belongings, few as they are; his backpack, still in the hall, held them all. A glance at his watch tells him he should heat the pizza. It is gone twelve o'clock.

'Hungry?'

Tyler has finished the picture he was working on. The colors make each shape stand out. He nods.

The man lifts down two plates to heat the pieces separately. 'Remember the time there was a fly trapped in the micro?' He opens the door for Tyler's, having changed the setting to high. 'We couldn't figure out where the buzzing came from. It sounded like the whole thing was about to explode. Amazing that it survived.'

'It hit the window like a bullet.' The kid's eyes sparkle. 'The fastest fly in the world.'

They had searched the floor afterwards but found no trace of it. Perhaps it had ended up on one of the strips of flypaper that hung in the kitchen well into September.

'Here's yours.' The man has shifted book and pens to the side. He slides the plate down in front of the boy, adding a knife and fork and a glass of water, to get him to tackle his food while he is in a good mood. He sets the timer for his own. 'Eat now.'

And the kid does.

But halfway through, he interrupts himself.

'Your name's not Detroit, is it?'

'No.'

'Mike's brother says it's a place.'

'It is.'

Tyler pokes at the corner of his mouth with the fork.

'So why does Mom call you Detroit?'

149

'She'd seen some program about it.'

'Detroit.'

'It was just an idea she had.'

The kid gives him a blank look but doesn't pursue the matter. They finish their meal in silence. Having cleared the table, the man washes the dishes, dries them, puts them away. Tyler has disappeared. He finds him in his room, staging a fight between a knight and a dinosaur.

'Let's go for a walk,' he suggests.

They set off down the road, past the abandoned farmhouse, their nearest neighbor, where he'd cut a few twigs of lilac after a row, a conciliatory gesture that brought its own reward. Now the bushes are empty of both flowers and leaves. 'You cold?' he asks.

Tyler shakes his head.

The man slows down; the kid, he realizes, is half running.

They pass the barn, which looks more derelict than the house; it must be decades since it was last used. A circular wire corncrib at its side, a giant birdcage, is equally deserted. This part of Wisconsin is old farming country with little to recommend it, except to the die-hard few.

They move on to the Anderson place.

Having returned on his own, relieved of his charge, the man debates with himself what else he could have done, but finds no feasible alternative. Besides, where is the harm? He'd sensed the instant they approached the house that the kid had known what was coming. He must have been left with the Andersons before. He will be fine until Lauren is back.

And she? He tightens the straps on his backpack and hikes it onto his shoulder. A heave, and it is in place. He opens the door. For her, relief will be mixed with a sense of guilt, where the blame will ultimately fall on him — more easily if he is gone.

The kid, when he left, wouldn't look at him. His lips had moved. 'What was that?' the man had asked, unable to make out the words. 'Will you still be Detroit?' was what he heard. But Tyler chose not to repeat it.

Detroit. As the house recedes behind him, it comes to him that

150

he never was. Whichever view you took, he wasn't it. He shrugs, then quickens his step. Ahead lies the road by which he had arrived. He will go on from there. Traveling frees the mind when you have no set destination.

In the Dark

*by **Richard Hooton***
(Fifth Place, Highly Commended)

EVERYTHING'S dark. Pitch black. *Where am I?* I can't move. My eyes won't open. *What the hell?*

I've been buried alive with mounds of suffocating earth slowly crushing me. I have to get out. Wait. There's no pressure; nothing's weighing me down. It's like floating in space with no stars.

It's not real. Just a nightmare. My alarm clock will sound, I'll awake, laugh with relief, then make a cup of tea and my world will be right again.

But I'm thinking too much to be asleep. I've always been afraid of the dark; anything could be lurking out there. Come on, Sarah, open your eyes. After 40 years of instantly obeying me, my body rebels. My mind screams "move", yet I'm frozen.

I yell. Silence mocks my pathetic efforts to make noise. So that's it. I see nothing. Feel nothing. I am nothing. I'm dead. *Is this it?* An immobile black silence. Am I in hell? Purgatory?

All I know is that I'm alone.

There's a noise. *I can hear.* It's rhythmic: a deep, whistling whoosh then a pause. There's a quiet beeping in the background and a mechanism that wheezes and clunks. It's like the world's most musically challenged orchestra; completely in time, never missing a beat, but with no melody or tune.

In their moments of silence I can hear the beat of my heart. It's faint, but life is pumping through my veins. My head's as fuzzy as radio static. I smell antiseptic and bleach. And something fainter. A sweet, delicate fragrance: the subtle notes of my favourite roses. I have senses. Am I blind and paralysed? I've read about locked-in conditions: A fully functioning mind trapped inside a broken-down body. Am I confined inside a personal hell?

I long to know; but I'm afraid of the truth.

I lie here — what choice do I have? — and wait. *How did I get here?* I piece together the jigsaw from fragments of memory.

152

Rushing to an appointment; always rushing, from one place to the next, one duty to another. I remember a letter; ominous black words on smooth, white paper. I dropped my four-year-old son off at nursery. How could I have forgotten Joey? Is it still morning? I think of his forlorn face when I don't arrive to pick him up, thinking his mummy has abandoned him.

I will myself to move. It's futile. I'm lost in the dark.

What's that? A new noise. A tapping that gets louder. Closer. Footsteps. A muttering, like someone talking through cloth, then it's clearer. They'll rescue me, surely?

'Five more minutes then I'm off.' A voice from my left. A woman's soft tones enlivened by eagerness. *They must see me.*

'Where you off tonight?' Another female voice. To my right. *Why aren't they doing something?*

'Round the pubs in town then I'll hit the clubs. Can't wait.' A night out. Excitement. Entertainment. Pleasure. *I'm trapped in a black tomb.*

'You ready? On the count.' Ready for what? 'One, two, three.'

A sensation, like I'm flying. Am I soaring up to meet my maker after all? Then back down. I think I'm stationary again.

The footsteps resume, then fade until they're gone. Just the noise of the machine is left. I'm as helpless as a trussed animal in a slaughterhouse. I can't rush now. All I can do is think about how I wish I could kiss Joey's feather-soft hair and breathe in his sweet scent. My little firework. To feel warm sunshine on my skin and be dazzled by its brightness. How sweetly frail like spun sugar those cherished moments seem now. All I have in my cocoon are memories.

There's footsteps again. A familiar musky scent in the air stirs me. Voices. This time male.

'I'm afraid there's been no change.' The tone is serious, sombre. 'I conducted the most basic reflex tests.' A nervous cough. 'But there was no response.' That fragrance. *Is it?*

'There must be more you can do?'

The voice chimes in my heart like a clapper striking a bell. Deep, masculine and as familiar to me as my name. It *is* him.

153

Pete, my husband of twenty years, my lighthouse, is by my side. His aftershave is comforting, his voice reassuring. Help is here. And he'll have made sure Joey's safe.

'We've done all we can.' What are they contemplating? 'It's been three days now.' I've been lying here that long? 'I'm sorry.' The stranger's voice is quiet and burdened with sadness. 'There's no chance of recovery.'

If my body could shake it would. Clearly, I'm in a hospital bed and the stranger's a doctor. It's a life or death conversation. *My life or death*. And I can't intervene. I want to shout out, to throw my arms into the air. All I can do is listen to them discuss my existence. Tell him, Pete. There's *always* hope. *Never* give up.

'It's too soon. She needs more time.' He does as I ask. But his voice drips with fear, sounds strangled by panic. You need to convince him, Pete.

'It's possible your wife's mental ability has been impaired by the lack of oxygen while we were restarting her heart. It may have caused catastrophic brain damage.' Why can't they tell there's nothing wrong with my mental ability? 'Consider her wishes. Would she want to be kept alive on a ventilator?'

I bloody well do want to be kept alive.

What's happened to me? I must think harder to shine a light through the fog. I remember pins and needles in my legs, still managing to get Joey to nursery before work, a pain snaking up me. I collapsed, recovered, went to the doctors, then hospital. That letter casts a shadow. The doctor gave it me, it described some condition, something about the immune system attacking the nervous system, leaving your brain unable to control your muscles. I was waiting at hospital. Then darkness.

I wonder what I look like, laid flat, all ghostly white in a hospital bed. Not too revolting, I hope. I imagine myself angel-like, long blonde hair flowing backwards against a crisp, white pillow, my complexion pale but clear.

The doctor said I'd had a heart attack. I must be in a coma but somehow able to hear. It's quiet. Pete hasn't answered the question. What's there to think about? I picture my husband, his stance: legs together, back straight, head bowed, hand on chin, contemplating.

He'll be as alone as I am; though we're just inches apart.

Our futures hang in this moment.

'We have to be realistic about your wife's prospects.' The doctor's voice is matter-of-fact grim. 'I think it's time to turn the machine off.' I see my danger. My life support. Keep that machine on, Pete.

'We did talk.' I've never heard Pete's voice so low, as if it's scraping the earth. Then I know what he's going to say. Please don't recall that conversation.

'About the right to die.' He gulps, near chokes on the words. 'Sarah said if she was permanently incapacitated she'd no longer want to live.'

If I could cry, I would. It's exactly what I said. But this *isn't* that situation. I try to scream out. I wish I could open my eyes. I can't bear this darkness. There must be some way of getting their attention, just the slightest movement: the flutter of an eyelid or trembling hand. Despite terror gripping my mind, my body remains still.

My death is sealed.

I'll never see Joey's bright eyes, burning with energy, again. I won't be there to catch him when he falls, to guide him, to teach him. I'll never see him grow, flourish, achieve. I'll have left him and Pete behind. For one last time I want to tell them I love them. They're all I've ever wanted in life – now I have nothing. Now I stop to appreciate. Why does it have to be dark to see the light?

And alone, inside your head, is the darkest place I've ever known.

Then Pete speaks. 'I still think she should be given more time. I've a feeling she can pull through.'

For the first time, I'm so happy Pete's going against my wishes. Relief isn't an adequate word. Time is all I need. If my mind is functioning my body will follow. It's up to the doctor now. Is his silence hesitation?

'I'll book Sarah in for an MRI scan to see what brain function there is and keep her on the ventilator until then.'

A lifeline. I know the scan will reveal me and they'll bring me

155

round. I can't wait to open my eyes and see my two boys again. I'll kiss my husband. I'll hold my son in my arms until they ache and breathe in his heavenly scent. Whatever it takes, I will rise and walk away from this hospital bed.

I'll be out of the darkness and into the light.

Lightning Source UK Ltd.
Milton Keynes UK
UKOW04f2133161017
311087UK00001B/100/P